The

The Loft

MARLEN HAUSHOFER

Translated into English by
AMANDA PRANTERA

QUARTET BOOKS

First published in 2011 by
Quartet Books Limited
A member of the Namara Group
27 Goodge Street, London WIT 2LD

Die Mansarde © Ullstein Buchverlage GmbH, Berlin.
First published in 1969 by Claassen Verlag

A catalogue record for this book
is available from the British Library

ISBN   978 0 7043 7207 8

Typeset by Antony Gray
Printed and bound in Great Britain by
T J International Ltd, Padstow, Cornwall

Sunday

FROM OUR BEDROOM WINDOW we can see a tree that we never seem to be able to agree about. Hubert says it's an acacia. He pronounces it 'agacia' because that was the way his father pronounced it, who was from Görz. Whether all people from Görz pronounce it that way, or just Hubert's father, I don't know, could be either. Hubert loves acacias; in old fashioned novels, where words are given their just currency, their scent is described as sweet and intoxicating, and so it is – sweet and intoxicating – only it is no longer possible to say so using these words. But never mind, it'll go on being sweet and intoxicating so long as there's one nose left in the world able to smell it.

Anyway, this tree on the near side of the street – Hubert says it's an acacia. Not that he knows anything much about trees. He merely likes acacias because his father – when he was young Ferdinand, and not the old Ferdinand that I knew – used to walk down an avenue that was lined with them. I imagine him doing this, not alone but in the company of a young girl. She'd have carried a parasol, I think, and the parasol would have been made of yellow silk. And the scent we can no longer describe by its proper adjectives would have filled the world. A round, integral world that no longer exists. The old Ferdinand no longer exists either, but his son goes on maintaining that the tree outside our bedroom window is an acacia.

In reply I can only smile. For me the tree is either an elm or an aspen. Which shows that I too know very little about trees, even though I grew up in the country. That was a long time ago, however, and Lord knows where I had my eyes in those days.

I don't think it's very important to know the names of things as they're written in nature books. 'Beautiful tree' is quite a good enough description for me. Lots of birds whose names I don't know I just call redfeet or greenwings or whatnots, and mammals likewise: I simply call them furry animals. Long-eared, thick-tailed, round-nosed, silky-soft furry animals. It doesn't make much difference to them, after all; they don't feel slighted or come up with complaints. And I reckon it's much the same to the tree, too, what I call it. So, elm or aspen, whichever.

It doesn't even know I'm there. The most curious thing about it is that you can only see it in winter. The moment it starts vegetating and covers itself with leaves it becomes invisible; then abracadabra and there it is again, bare, its stripped twigs delicately etched against the grey November sky, and the guessing game over its name starts up afresh.

On this morning Hubert sat up in bed and said: 'It's definitely an agacia.'

'Elm or aspen,' I said, stubborn.

'You must think I'm daft,' said Hubert. 'Think I can't tell an agacia when I see one?'

I know perfectly well he hasn't a clue what an acacia looks like, but I don't say so, so as not to irritate him. I'm not too sure about what irritates him, really; sometimes he's pretty unrufflable, some-times he gets in a bait about nothing. This acacia business would certainly annoy him, like everything does that concerns his father. Secretly Hubert goes in for a bit of ancestor worship, and, since I do too, I'm careful on this point. I said nothing, let the matter drop and went on looking at the tree.

It's a Sunday in February, and this little scene takes place every Sunday morning. Weekdays we don't have time for these sorts of games.

'There's a bird on that tree,' Hubert reports. 'A starling.'

'Nonsense,' I say. 'There aren't any starlings in the winter, it'll be a blackbird.' I'm at a bit of a disadvantage here because Hubert is far sighted and I'm slightly the reverse. All I could see was a small black sploge in the fork of a branch.

6

'No,' says Hubert, 'it's definitely not a blackbird.'

'Maybe it's a greenfinch, then,' I suggest. I'm not quite sure what the birds that I call greenfinches are really called, they look like very big sparrows, only green.

'You and your greenfinches,' says Hubert scornfully and opens up his book – an account of the battle of St Gotthard-Mogersdorf in 1664. Ancient battles are his favourite reading matter and he sees himself as being a far better strategist than the musty old generals of the past. It's pathetic to see how worked up he gets, not being able to re-plan all our lost battles for us. It's not patriotism, I realized that long ago, but merely a burning quest for perfection. Everybody else's lost battles bother him just as badly. And yet this sort of reading seems paradoxically to soothe him, and since tons of books have been written on the subject he'll never run out of material. He could tranquilly afford to live to a hundred – although I don't think he will somehow, and I definitely hope for him that he won't.

Hubert's fifty two now, and in pretty good shape considering he does nothing for his health. His blood pressure is normal, his joints ache a bit now and then, four teeth are missing, which isn't a lot, and he's still got a good thatch of thickish brown hair, streaked, obviously, with a certain amount of grey. He smokes too much, I suppose, but hardly drinks at all and is what you'd call a frugal man all round, with a slight leaning towards the faddy. I don't know why it is he won't live to a great old age. Of course he works too hard, but he seems to enjoy it, so it can't be that bad for him.

He smiled and slid back in a cloud of acacia scent into the battle of St Gotthard-Mogersdorf, forgetting wife, tree, and bird on same.

The tree stood flat against the sky like a drawing on grey ricepaper. It does look a bit Chinese to tell the truth. If you stare at it for long it changes. At least it does if I do. The white-grey patches of light between the branches begin to bulge until they form so many soft balls, and soon the tree – elm or aspen as may be – holds the whole sky imprisoned in its silvery grey fingers.

Then if I close my eyes and open them a minute later the tree is flat again: a picture that makes you neither happy nor sad, but that I could go on staring at for hours. And as I do so, in a trice the mysterious process starts up again and the sky becomes round and re-enclosed by softly curving fingers.

The most remarkable thing about this tree, though, is that it can make your wishes explicit for you and grant them. Not that I have any particularly burning desires any more, but I have moods and worries, and things that annoy me, and all of these the tree draws out of me, beds them down in its branches, and then tucks them up in its balls of cloud until they melt away in the cool dampness. Then I can turn my head aside, light and empty, and go to sleep for another half hour. During this half hour I never dream. The tree, whether acacia, elm or aspen, is a dependable tree that you can rely on.

For this I am grateful, because nowadays it is a question of storing up strength, and then using this strength to get through life as gracefully as possible. It's beyond my powers to go throwing plates around, but on the other hand I don't want to end up becoming bitter and ironic – as I easily could, being slightly that way inclined. I don't want to brood either or mope or do what we Austrians call 'mocken'. The English word 'sulk' best describes this condition-to-be-avoided-at-all-costs. Moping ('schmollen' in German) sounds unforgivably twee, and brooding is in fact something quite different: a hermit can brood without giving offence to anyone, but I don't think I ever heard of one moping. 'Mocken' comes closer to the mark, suggesting as it does both the gloom and stupidity of people who go in for this activity. Sulk, however, says it all, and on top gives an idea of coldness and indifference, deliberately intended to wound the person at whom the sulk is directed. And I don't want to wound anybody. Round the world and round the clock, far too much wounding goes on as it is.

Hubert broods occasionally. But he broods discreetly, seated at his desk, his face shielded by a newspaper. Sometimes he even goes out to a café for this purpose. It would never cross my mind to accompany him there. If I feel like going out to a café I go alone. I'm not missing out on much: married couples can do practically everything together, but they can't sit in cafés reading newspapers since it straight away gives them the impression they are fed up to the teeth with one another.

Of course, sometimes Hubert and I *are* fed up to the teeth with one another, but as soon as we realise this we fall into a deep melancholy until the regrettable state of affairs has passed. We simply can't afford to be fed up with each other, because otherwise who can we turn to, who can act as a prop? All other people are strangers to us, even our friends, who are only really acquaintances anyway.

Even our daughter Ilse is a stranger: fifteen years old and not a clue what she's meant to do with us. She has the prettiest bedroom in the house because we like spoiling her and want her to be happy. She thrives magnificently and is a cheerful, well-adjusted youngster. Sometimes she reminds me of an aunt of mine who became a nun – although Ilse herself will never be a nun. Not that I can say that for sure, of course, when unexpected things happen all the time. It's a good thing for Ilse that we don't really need her or depend on her in any deep way. Ilse doesn't belong to the innermost circle. Before her birth something happened to make of her a child who is born after its parents' real life span is over. She is a posthumous child whose parents just happen to be still around, carrying on as if nothing had happened. Probably there are a lot of children like that, only you never get to hear about them. Despite being posthumous, however, I still think she's lucky. Her friends envy her because her parents only fuss over her when she herself wants them to. What other child can claim to be so fortunate?

Our son Ferdinand, named after Hubert's father, the elder Ferdinand, is not so lucky. I don't think he ever was lucky. He was born before that event that changed everything, and was always in the centre of our lives: there where the water is still, but where the least little wrong movement can send a body skidding off God knows where. He must have noticed that. Early on he must have discovered that it was better not to move too much and to be constantly on the watch. He is not a coward so he calls himself Ferdinand in full, even though this royal-sounding name let him in for a good deal of ragging at school. He's probably thankful that his grandfather wasn't called Leopold, as easily might have been the case. Since his twenty-first birthday, which was last year, he sub-rents a bed-sit in the ninth District. Ferdinand, you see, is something of an heir. Hubert's mother, the old Madam Magistrate, left him all her money. To him the money, and to Hubert the house – but this last only because it was it was his already, willed to him by his father, and she had tenancy. She left nothing to Ilse, not even a piece of jewellery, and obviously nothing to me either.

On Sundays Ferdinand often comes for a meal; sometimes he drops in for coffee on weekdays too, and he visits us as a matter of course on all main holidays such as Easter and Christmas and so forth. He didn't move out because he doesn't like us, but only because he wants to be free and independent. The old lady's money will see him through University, and when he's got his degree he can start earning some of his own. Hubert secretly minds a bit about this, but I'm pleased. It's a good thing for Ferdinand that he doesn't have to ask us for money, and can live under the impression of being a free man. Although I'm not sure he sets much weight by this superstition any more. He was always quick on the uptake. To have a grown up son around the place, who was born before that particular event and is lodged right in the heart of the maelstrom, would be an uncomfortable situation all round. The fact that he belongs to the innermost circle makes everyday living with him difficult. The nearness is overwhelming, and all three of us are chary of nearness.

Besides, Hubert and I are past helping, and nothing much can knock us off course any more, only the irrevocable destiny common to all mankind. It is a good thing therefore that Ferdinand has moved. Maybe sometimes he gets a bit homesick for the comforts of a bourgeois household, but he goes on living in his bed-sit, scorning the homesickness, and taking good care to stay in the centre where all is calm, and not to set so much as a foot in the danger zone.

And for him no zone is more dangerous than this house. Sometimes it must exasperate him – the fact that he daren't take that one step that would send him shooting off to the ends of the earth. So then he slams his study books shut and goes off to a movie or to see his friends. I have no idea how he gets on with girls. He has that certain charm about him which is probably guaranteed to attract just those bossy and ambitious types he should avoid.

Ilse, who takes after my mother, has a happy, uncomplicated nature. Perhaps Hubert could be happy too. The fact that he is not, lies not so much with him as with outside influences and circumstances that he was not brought up to cope with. Ferdinand takes after neither me nor Hubert, but his grandfather. In a strange way he will always be what people used to call 'a true gentleman'. He doesn't know this, of course, because you can't recognize things or situations that you haven't seen or experienced, but it is perfectly obvious that he can't be otherwise: Ferdinand, who stems from the early period of our lives, can only ever be an anachronism. We realise this and do not know whether to be pleased or sorry; in either case there is nothing we could do to change things. There is no way of changing anything: everything has happened and goes its own way, we can't lift so much as a finger. And as regards Hubert's feelings I'm only guessing anyway, because we hardly ever talk about our son, and certainly not in such a meaningful way. Ilse is a nice unproblematic subject of conversation – like all people are, whom one is fond of and at ease with, but who do not belong to the innermost circle.

Brother and sister hardly relate to one another at all. The age difference is too great. Ferdinand considers Ilse a silly little kid, which she definitely is not; and Ilse looks on Ferdinand as weird old fogey, which from her point of view is understandable.

Sometimes he brings her sweets or helps her with her Latin homework. We were a real family only for three years, namely from the moment of Ferdinand's birth until that event that we never talk about and that all three of us try to forget. And from time to time we do forget, totally; it is merely the after-effects that admit of no extinguishing.

And that's why I'm so glad that the tree snuffs out my memories for me, and I can sleep half an hour's dreamless sleep.

When I woke up again, the sun was breaking through the grey winter sky. Unless there's rain or snow it tries to do this every day, although it hardly ever succeeds. I find these efforts rather moving. It sits there behind the smog like a big red disc and throws a peculiar pink light over the city. It makes the tree glitter with moisture, and transforms its branches into silver and copper. When that happens I can hardly believe that it's a real tree, with roots in the earth, and sap oozing through it even in winter. It doesn't look like an organic thing any more; it becomes an artefact, hard and shiny as glass.

'Remarkable,' said Hubert, and laid the battle of St Gotthard-Mogersdorf aside. 'Quite remarkable. Every time a bird hops onto that branch, another one flies off it.'

'Perhaps it's some kind of ritual,' I said gratuitously.

'What are we going to do today?' Hubert asked.

At this I felt a little jab inside, nothing painful, just the smarting of an old wound. With his question he shifted the responsibility for the day onto me: Here, see if you can't make something halfway agreeable out of it, seeing that on a Sunday I simply can't go to the office. You don't have to put yourself out much; I'm sure you'll think up something.

It is a game – one of the few we have left. I prefer not to think about the ones we used to play in the past. Since nothing new comes into my mind I am obliged to give thought to the matter. In fact I always give the matter thought because I am anxious we should not hit a wrong note. A wrong note would trouble me for hours or even days, and I can't afford to let this happen.

Ilse was away on a ski-course with her classmates. (Hardly an issue because even when she's here she prefers to spend Sunday afternoons with her friends rather than with us.) What with cooking and tidying up, the morning would pass. We hardly ever go out to a restaurant because it drives us crazy having to sit and wait for ages until they bring the bill. Plus which, the food is dreadful, even in expensive places; and we don't like the smells either, or the other eaters, who sit far too close. Only the afternoon, therefore, needed planning: you can't always just read or play records.

'There's an exhibition of modern French painters,' I said limply.

Hubert just grunted.

'What about Finnish furniture?' I said.

'Hideous,' said Hubert.

'A stroll, then,' I suggested, 'and afterwards a Swedish film.'

'The Swedes depress me,' said Hubert.

They depress me too, so I went along with him on this. 'I don't really like going to the cinema anyway,' I said, 'films are so creepy.'

'In what way?' Asked Hubert.

'I don't like all those giant faces,' I said. 'Everything is so huge, I find it physically disturbing. I'm scared of giants. When was the last time we went, do you remember?'

Hubert thought for a moment: he is the memory bank of our marriage. 'Seven months ago,' he said. 'Some comic thing or other.'

I remembered then. 'It was not at all comic,' I said. 'All those dreadful big heads on the screen. Like being among cannibals. They open their mouths so wide and have too many teeth, and facial lines like ravines, and the women all wear false eyelashes – the whole thing is quite obscene. Even the lovers look like ogres. It scared me no end.'

Hubert went to the trouble of actually turning his head to look at me. His eyes are grey, and once upon a time they used to seem to me bright and full of life. Now they looked like water under a layer of ice. I could see something wiggling under the ice: tiny little fishes against the background of a frozen lake. 'Strange,' he said, 'I don't remember anything about that myself. When you're scared, you breathe much faster. I notice that straight away as a rule, and I didn't notice it then at all.'

'You were all caught up in the film. And you were laughing, I remember that perfectly – that's why you didn't notice.'

'But you never used to be scared of the cinema,' he said.

'It must come from watching television,' I put in quickly. 'When you're so used to dwarves, you probably can't take giants any more.'

'Well, that settles it then,' Hubert decided. 'No cinema.'

'I don't suppose we want to go and pay anyone a visit, do we?' I asked.

Hubert made no reply – it would have been pointless anyway: my question was not meant seriously. We never visit anybody unless we can't help it. We have few acquaintances, and none of them in common; we don't have relatives either, and if we did, we would be unlikely to visit them.

I could tell I was approaching a whirlpool that might easily catch me up in its vortex. I had no intention of being caught: the game had to last for a certain amount of time, and this time had not yet expired.

'Window shopping?' I said.

Hubert laughed. His laugh had a slightly unpleasant ring to it, a bit gurgley and insidious. Deep down there is a malicious streak in him that rarely comes to the surface. In the old days I used even to like it. It added a touch of excitement to life. Now all this laugh says is: I know you inside out, my love. And I don't want to be known inside out.

'OK, then,' I said submissively: 'I reckon we go to the War Museum.'

At that Hubert lay back on his pillow, contented, and reopened his book.

Always, when we are at a loss what to do on a Sunday afternoon, we go to the War Museum. We behave as though it were a last resort, but in reality we don't want to go anywhere else. In Hubert's case I can see why he visits it so willingly; in mine the reasons are less clear, but the fact remains that I do. I prefer the War Museum to any other museum or gallery, and indeed my fondness for it is perhaps slightly worrying.

I gave a last quick look at the tree: the sun had given up, worn out by it efforts, and the pink light had gone out. I got up and left the room.

After lunch we went for an hour's walk. The weather was cloudy, cold and still. I liked that, because the prevailing wind that normally blows in this city gets me down. We spoke of nothing in particular and were very friendly and happy together. But then that's the way we nearly always are. In fact, always are. I didn't know that the next morning my life would change in the most extraordinary way, and neither did Hubert. I doubt he ever will; I hope not, anyway.

Later we drove to the War Museum in the car. It's nice, driving, even in February; although not as nice as in summer, when on Sundays the city lies there like a dead town, smelling of hot asphalt.

Hubert bought himself, straight away in the foyer, a booklet on the battle of Ebelsberg, 1809, and a postcard with a portrait of Prince Eugene, painted by Johann Kupetsky. The card will disappear into his writing desk and never get written, because who would Hubert ever send a postcard to? Then off he went to peer into the showcases containing photographs from the First World War. He's convinced, you see, that among these old photographs he has spotted one of his father. I can't really pronounce on this: all I can see is a gaunt young man in the uniform of a Lieutenant, with puttees and a cap with a turned-up peak, who is staring, tired and thoughtful, at a machine gun. The picture was taken somewhere in the South Tyrolean Alps and is already yellowing. I only saw Hubert's father three times in all and he was over sixty by then. It could be him, naturally, but there must have been a lot of young men of roughly the same aspect.

The moment we reach the showcases Hubert forgets about me entirely. I go ahead slowly on my own, wandering through the familiar rooms. I stop to look at the dummies in their old military uniforms: they look so life-like in their glass cases, it makes you start. When you observe them closer, of course, they look neither alive nor dead – just dolls, with that mixture of the attractive and sinister that dolls have. I always linger in front of them. They fascinate me. The whole War Museum is in fact an attractive and sinister place, and perhaps that's what I like about it. I visit the Radetzky Room, the Duke Karl Room and the Prince Eugene room and marvel to myself at the incredible cleanliness and order that prevail. No other museum in the city is so lovingly looked after and cherished. It seems odd, but when you think of it, this is natural and indeed enlightening.

My wanderings ended as usual at the tent of Kara Mustapha – the big Turkish tent. There I sat down and took a rest. I knew that outside, the cars were crossing over the ring-road, and traffic lights were blinking; and with an uneasy stab I realised that I felt more at home in this friendly reign of the dead than in the living city. Although I'm not sure either whether the city really is alive, or whether it is just a marshalling place for dummies who are allowed to trot around a bit before being shut up in their cases like the old halberdiers I'd just been looking at.

I like being surrounded by things that don't notice me or come near me. Models of old ships with billowing sails no wind ever fills, and rows of flags and standards that once meant everything, and now mean nothing except brittle silk that crumbles at the touch. It smelt of great age here, of leather and fusty material, and also of floor wax.

After Hubert and I had met up again – the tent is our customary meeting place – we made our way slowly downstairs in silence. I knew that we didn't belong here but outside, with the cars and traffic lights, in a world that isn't ours either, or not by choice.

Nevertheless the quiet of the past, and its fading glimmer, exercised over me a great power of attraction. The past always does, even those periods which we find hateful or repugnant; in fact we only find them hateful and repugnant on account of this power.

'Did you recognize him today?' I asked.

'I'm pretty convinced now that I did,' Hubert said. 'It's definitely his bearing. Only of course I'll never be quite sure.'

'No,' I said, 'you'll never be quite sure.'

Then we spoke no more about the matter. The afternoon in the War Museum had passed and we were standing in the street. It had begun to snow, in small silent flakes, and the air was cold and smelt clean. On the way home we stayed silent. Hubert had to concentrate because the road was slippery and one of our wipers doesn't work properly. I could only see out through a blur; plus which, it was nearly dark and the oncoming headlights blinded me.

The short yellow grass of our front lawn was already covered by a thin layer of snow, and the sight of it reminded me of something. I couldn't remember what, though, and in the end gave up trying.

The house was nice and warm and smelt slightly of smoke – a smell you can never really get rid of. But it smelt of tangerine peel too, bits of which were lying on the table, and this smell was not so bad at all. Hubert made off to his room, and I knew he would now read the battle of St Gotthard-Mogersdorf to its end. On weekdays he hardly has time to read, at least never as much as he would like.

I reckoned that would take care of him for a while, so I climbed up to the loft and sat down at my drawing board. The loft belongs to me. Even Hubert only comes there when explicitly invited. That happens seldom and is more of a ritual than anything else. When he, for example, entrusts me with a rare confidence, and I know he's feeling uncomfortable on this account, I counter-balance by showing him one of my secrets in return. My secrets are tiny and worthless – mostly drawings of reptiles or birds – but

I have nothing else to offer. And since Hubert's confidences are nothing very special either, everything works out fine and balance is restored.

In the loft I can draw or paint, or if I feel like it, simply prowl up and down – a habit that would get on Hubert's nerves. I've inherited just this one talent with which there's not a great deal that I can do. There was a time I used to illustrate books, but that was ages ago now. Hubert wouldn't like me to earn money that way, even if the sums were small. Especially now that Ferdinand needs nothing from him any more. I'm glad I'm not fettered by the terms of a commission and can draw what I like.

My talent is very limited, but inside these narrow limits I have become somewhat of a master. I have always drawn, and after leaving school I did a two year course of graphics. From it I learnt all I could, but strictly speaking it wasn't all that necessary. I have never drawn anything else except insects, fish, reptiles and birds, and have never attempted mammals or humans. I could draw flowers as well, if I wanted to, but somehow I never have.

For the past few years I have concentrated almost entirely on birds. I have a precise aim in view, although I can't imagine what I would do afterwards if ever I reached it. Perhaps that's one of the reasons I never get that far. My aim is to draw a bird that is not the only bird in the world. By this I mean that anyone looking at it must grasp this fact straight away. To date I have never achieved this and I doubt I ever shall. Sometimes I think I'm on the right track, but the next day I look at the drawing again and see that the bird in question hasn't a clue there exist other members of its species apart from itself; so then I take the drawing and shut it away in a drawer. There are stacks of other lonely birds in there already – pictures that no one but myself has ever set eyes on. Only Hubert has seen a few of them, but to him they are all little masterpieces: he doesn't realise they've all come out wrong. Now and again I see a glimmer of hope, but very seldom. Many years ago, before I got so hooked on birds, I once drew a starling that looked as if it was listening to the far-off call of another starling from a neighbouring garden. Something in the way it held its head and fluffed out its feathers seemed to indicate this. But it was only a faint echo of a call that it heard; no real recognition of a fellow creature. All the same, at the time it made me very happy. This little drawing got lost in the war.

A few days earlier I had started on a swallow, but from the outset I could tell it was not a good choice. Because you always see swallows in flocks you imagine that they're sociable birds, but not a bit of it: all they do is flash in front of one another with nothing on their minds but food. My swallow, at any rate, looked extremely chuffed with her deliberately chosen solitude: a decorative little creature with not a thought of other swallows in her little feathery head. I worked on her for ten minutes or so: a change of line here, a spot of colour there. Then I stood up again and started walking up and down. It's a good thing the loft is over the kitchen: like that I don't disturb Hubert. And it's important for me to be free to pace – from the table to the fireplace and back again, then to the chest of drawers, then the sofa, and finally to the window.

From the window I can see the wall of our neighbours' house – a very ugly grey wall. This is good too, because it can't distract me. My fingers twitched a bit, the way they always do when I forbid them to draw. I shut my eyes and saw before me the swallow as I wanted her to be. Immediately I rushed to the table and altered her eyes slightly. Now she looked really provoking, ready to burst from the sheer joy of her solitude. There never was such a cheeky swallow; she seemed to be mocking me. From the look in her eye she now appeared to be shrieking out, 'I'm the only swallow in the world and thank God for that!' It made me so cross that I tore the paper into little bits and threw them in the wastepaper basket: I wasn't going to have this little monster surviving, not even in the drawer.

Again something had gone wrong and in a particularly irritating way. I went back to my pacing, and suddenly I realised that the fault must lie with me; evidently I wanted to draw nothing but solitary birds. This realisation set me thinking for a long time, but it didn't help one bit. Eventually I had to admit to myself that today I could begin nothing new, and with this I went downstairs and back into the living room.

Hubert was sitting in front of the TV, watching a sports programme. He's not that keen on sport, but he seldom misses this particular programme. He watches too much television really, and since he doesn't like watching alone, I also waste a lot of time this way. He hardly notices me, never talks to me either, but wants me to be there in the room with him. Sometimes I read as I sit there, but the dim light is bad for the eyes. Television is also bad for the eyes, for that matter. Basically, everything we do is bad for something, and if we were to follow all the advice on the subject the only really healthy activity would be to be dead.

But anyway, there we sat till eleven, and I can't remember having seen anything at all. I must have done, because I kept my eyes open all the time, facing in the direction of the screen. Where are all the days and months and years gone that I have wasted in this way? The thought of having all this knowledge inside me of which I have no memory at all is creepy. It's like sitting in a peaceful glade without an inkling that any single minute a wild beast may spring out from behind a bush. I do not like surprises.

Monday

The post always arrives round about nine, bringing nothing but ads as a rule, or else magazines I have subscribed to in a weak moment. Bills and business letters are all delivered straight to Hubert's office. If any other kind of mail were to reach him there too I would never know about it, but I think it unlikely he has any kind of private correspondence. He has no relatives left except for an uncle in Trieste, who is a very old man now and sends us just a greetings card every Christmas; all Hubert's acquaintances live here in the city and can therefore keep in touch by phone. No, I can't imagine anyone writing him a letter.

I get no private mail either. My only living relation, a sister of my mother, lives in a convent in the Tyrol. I don't even know for sure that she is still alive as I've never heard from her since she entered it. Maybe her Order is so strict that she not allowed any contact with the outside world. Maybe she prays for me now and then. This is a weird but comforting thought. Or maybe she's simply forgotten I exist.

On this particular Monday morning, however, a letter for me arrived. A thick yellow envelope with the address in capital letters. No sender's name. I took it into the kitchen with me and eyed it warily. Circled round it like a cat round a saucer of scalding milk.

Finally I slit the envelope, and out came a pair of yellowing pages from a school copybook, thickly covered in a hand that I recognized straight away. It was my own writing; by which I mean it was the writing of a young person who once had been me. I knew not only the handwriting, I knew exactly what it was I was looking at, even though it was almost seventeen years since last I'd seen it. I felt nothing but aversion and the slight wave of shock that unexpected events always cause me. I crammed the pages back into the envelope and took it up to the loft with me, where I slipped the thing into a drawer under a pile of sketching paper. It's not my way to hide things as a rule but this one needed hiding: it contained nothing offensive or damaging but it was a relic from a past I did not want to be reminded of.

This done, I went down again to the kitchen, determined not to let the interruption interfere with my routine: thoughts and objects from my loft-life have no right to spill over into the rest of the house. I'm not a very disciplined person but this is a rule I always abide by.

So I went back to my housework, which seemed in the meantime to have suddenly become immensely important. I grabbed hold of my big wooden spoon and concentrated uniquely on the task in hand: the baking of a nut-roll. A proper nut-roll calls for time and attention so it kept me occupied for quite a while.

At midday Hubert came home and we sat down together to lunch. I still had this groggy feeling, as if someone had bashed me on the head. Hubert didn't notice because he dived into his newspaper straight away, and we don't talk much at meals anyway. When he'd finished his paper he lay down on the sofa in the living room for twenty minutes or so, and I cleared up and set the kitchen to rights again. I always have to do this promptly because it's a task I particularly dislike and I need to get it over with.

When Hubert had gone back to his office I had a scan through the paper myself. That is, I behaved as if I was having a scan through it; what I was really doing during this time, I have no idea.

At three o'clock Ferdinand turned up to fetch a couple of books. He is tall, and has to stoop when he kisses me. His cheek smelt nice – young and vital. He's taller than his father – in this too he takes after his grandfather. I made some coffee and put the nut-roll on the table. I have a theory Ferdinand possesses a secret sense that enables him to smell nut-roll and the like across the breadth of the entire city: it's a fact that he always turns up punctually every time I bake a cake.

'Everything okay with you two?' He asked.

'Much as usual,' I said. 'Your father's having trouble with his corns again, and I haven't been sleeping all that well.'

'Why not?' Ferdinand asked.

'I don't know,' I replied. 'Perhaps I dream too deeply. Probably a question of growing old.'

'Nonsense,' said Ferdinand. 'You look as young as ever.'

He's very convincing when he says things like that. I immediately felt young and pretty. He studied me thoughtfully through his big black eyes. His hair, also black, sprung off his forehead clean and shiny, and he reminded me of a nocturnal bird I once drew. I always think of him as having been darkish blond up to his third birthday, with blue eyes, but that obviously can't have been the case: hair can go on growing darker, but at that age eyes don't change their colour any more. I have a lot of false memories of this kind; I shouldn't wonder if all my memories were false, they easily might be. Ferdinand's complexion has lost its childhood rosy tan, and is now pale with a touch of olive – a very clear and even skin-tint, unusual in these parts. He has absorbed like a sponge all the darkness of those far-off, murky days.

Poor Ferdinand, you can never really tell whether he's happy to be alive or not. When I was his age I had already lost my grandfather – or what was left of his former self, that is, which was not a great deal. I was alone in this city, a long way away from the grassy banks and meadows of the Danube, and, as far as I knew, forever. A long way, too, from the broad-beamed house, and the little village of Rautersdorf, which is still marked on the map. I had very little money left. In those days I was very unhappy. It was not until I met Hubert, a bit later on, that I started to know happiness again. And it lasted, let's say, from when I was twenty-four until I was twenty-nine. During that time I still had hardly any money, very few clothes, no house of my own, but I had a husband and a son. Nothing drew my attention away from them: neither the setting up of the household nor its day by day organization – clothes, curtains, laundry, shopping and so forth.

Especially not cooking, for there was practically no food to cook. Most of our friends were no better off, a few were even worse. But we were all healthy and full of hope, and there were always a lot of little children around. Hubert, who had got his degree and was now studying for the bar, sold his camera, and his father's fishing rods and guns, and also a radio and a microscope. The old Ferdinand had died shortly before our wedding. He used to wear a deep black moustache, and his eyebrows had grown together over his nose, which lent him a rather gloomy aspect. In youthful photographs he looked like an Anarchist who carries an elegant little bomb in his coat pocket. Whereas in reality he was a very kind man, who never spoke so much as a cross word to his wife, which in my opinion places him among the saints. He ended his career by being a High Court Magistrate, and the name Ferdinand suited him very well.

Hubert studied law too, not because his father forced him to, but because all branches of study were much the same to him, and law was, so to speak, close to hand. He sold not only his father's fishing tackle and gun, but also his dinner jacket and his dress overcoat with the fur collar. Each time he went to visit his mother he would manage to prise one or other of these things from her; in theory they belonged to him already but in practise she was loath to part with them. That woman had difficulty in parting with anything, whether it was her own property or not. There were rows between mother and son. She also objected to having been obliged to hand over her son to a woman she didn't like. No reflection on me really, because she hardly liked anybody.

In truth there was little to reproach me for. I came from a respectable family, even though I was the only member of it left. I had inherited a little money, and if it hadn't outlasted the war that was not my fault. Admittedly my parents had both contracted tuberculosis, but I myself was healthy: a nice warm pink complexion and a mass of dark blond hair. Madam Magistrate didn't even know the truth about my parents either: Hubert had told her that my father had died of flu, and my mother of pneumonia.

Had I not been so blindly in love with him, that reticence of his should have acted as a warning.

But I accepted everything in those days without question. I didn't want to be alone any longer; I wanted urgently to start a family, and to sit with them round me every evening under the lamp like my grandfather used to do, strong and solid and pivotal like him, and tell them stories. Overlooking, of course, the fact that I was neither strong nor solid, nor could I act as pivot to anyone, nor tell stories – or not the kind of stories, anyway, that a family would like to hear. I was painting a false picture of myself and of Hubert too. Had I been the way I fancied I was, Hubert's insecurity would never have been able to damage us, and neither would his mother. I would have dealt with her in a trice. But since I was inexperienced in those days and couldn't recognise the truth, things soon began to go wrong. All the same, I put in a lot of effort in that period. I even earned some extra money of my own, illustrating books and designing greetings cards. Admittedly, I could only paint plants and insects, birds and fish, but for certain books that was enough. On one occasion, when we really needed the cash, I had a go at doing Christmas cards, but the angels came out looking like a flight of owls, and the Baby Jesus resembled a swaddled carp. Reluctantly I had to drop this plan. However I was full of good will, perhaps too much so. My butterflies were in constant demand, and if only for this reason Madam Magistrate might have seen fit to treat me for once like a human being, but she treated me as if I simply didn't exist. Today this wouldn't bother me in the slightest, but at that time a little show of warmth might have done me good. It was not forthcoming, though. Hubert did his utmost to play the role of the confident young father, and I took his confidence for real. In this, without meaning to, I did him a wrong.

In my opinion Hubert must have loved his mother very much as a small child, but then decided later on that he didn't like her, and began to quarrel with her from that moment on. It was then that he suddenly discovered his father and became strongly attached to him. This was long before I turned up on the scene, so I had nothing to do with the worsening relationship to his mother; in fact it used to distress me that he visited her so seldom and was so standoffish towards her. Later, when he realised he had let me down and betrayed me, he punished his mother for this, hard. He hardly ever went to see her any more and became cold and distant. He couldn't punish himself directly, but he did so indirectly, through her. Then there came a time when the old lady tried to establish contact with me. When Ilse was born, she gave me a pearl necklace. I wasn't particularly pleased but I thanked her politely. It was too late: she understood this and made no further approach. I never wore the necklace, not because it came from Madam Magistrate, but simply because I don't like wearing jewellery. When Ilse turns eighteen I will give it to her for her birthday.

Ferdinand pushed the nut-roll away from him and said, 'I can't eat any more, Mum. It was fantastic, but I can't eat any more. How's poor old Fini getting on?'

Fini is Hubert's mother's one-time cook, Serafine. She lives in an old people's home, but has been in hospital now for some weeks. I go and visit her occasionally. She means nothing to me at all: when she was slave to Madam Magistrate she hardly even noticed me. Hubert sends her money but never goes to see her; it's only Ferdinand who bothers about her to some degree. He was the only one, too, who used to visit his grandmother regularly, and who was genuinely fond of her. Strangely enough, she never tried to boss him around. I think she must have loved him; hence her leaving him all the money.

'Fini's a bit better now,' I said. 'In a couple of weeks she'll be able to leave.'

'I must go and pay her a visit,' said Ferdinand. 'She's a poor old worm.'

The description was exact. I marvel at Ferdinand for the patience he shows towards poor old worms. He's got more heart than his parents. I'm sure he will visit me in hospital when the time comes. His greatest gift is that of giving people around him the feeling that they are important and cherished. I have no idea how he does it or whether any play acting is involved, but it is so pleasant you soon shelve your doubt.

'By the way,' he added, looking at me with his dark eyes, 'I've seen something that might come in useful: a little foam cushion that you can fit over corns. I'll get one for Dad.' I felt ashamed: it's always my son who comes up with ideas like this, never me. I never pay attention to window displays.

'Been having bad dreams lately, then?' He asked.

'Not really,' I said, 'just tiring ones. For example, I have to clean out a house that's full of filth, and when I wake up I feel exactly as if I'd worked the whole night long.'

'Doesn't sound much fun,' said Ferdinand, 'but it doesn't surprise me. You work too hard, that's what. This house will be the end of you. Time you got yourself a helper.'

'I'll give you some nut-roll to take away with you.' I said to divert his attention. I wanted to avoid entering a discussion on this point. I know why it is I don't want any house help: I'm not sociable enough to put up with having a cleaner around. So it serves me right; if I get tired, it's my own fault. And anyway, at my age any form of physical activity can only do me good.

Ferdinand tactfully dropped the subject. He probably looks on both of us – his father and myself – as hopeless cases: a couple of soon-to-be old worms whom you have to be kind to because they are past changing. 'Udo and Fritz asked to be remembered to you,' he said.

I had to stop and think for a minute, and when I'd conjured up the two young men in question it struck me as unlikely that either of them had ever given me a thought. However, I thanked warmly and sent greetings back.

Ferdinand grinned. The grin was slightly twisted and I liked him for it: he had seen through my bluff. He wiped his mouth, stood up and kissed me on the cheek, so lightly I could hardly feel it, and said, 'Got to rush, Mum, thanks for the delicious grub, and take a bit more care of yourself.'

Rushing was hardly the right word: all Ferdinand's movements are extremely languid. I watched him from the window, and he waved at me and ambled off towards the tram. Only now did I realise how cleverly he had avoided saying one single word about his own circumstances. He is a master at that. Udo and Fritz asked to be remembered to you – he likes bestowing amiable little qualities on his friends. Without this self-generated aura of warmth, life probably seems unbearable to him. He smears everyday life with a drop of oil, so as not to hear its squeaking and creaking and be offended by it. Ferdinand is musical and has a sensitive ear for dissonance. In the face of his melancholy disposition he moves elegantly and lightly through the world.

I followed him with my eyes, my wise, grownup son, who has grasped perfectly that it is better for us to suffer a little under his absence than to be reminded constantly, by his presence, of the time when we were a happy, unified whole. Not that it is likely he can remember that far back, but he has grasped it all the same.

Ilse is not wise. She goes rigid with boredom and distaste when she's with people she doesn't like. She doesn't need to be wise; she will always do exactly what she wants, regardless of others. She is not musical either: a bit of squeaking and creaking doesn't bother her at all. I never have to worry about Ilse, she has already got to where I have never reached and never will. Her confidence often takes my breath away. Ilse belongs to my mother's side of the family: foresters and farmers, people made of milk and blood – blond, blue-eyed and sure of themselves, and sometimes a bit short tempered. No-nonsense people, people who can be rough mannered but at bottom are good-natured and generous. I know the kind very well because I grew up with them – in my grandfather's house, which was my first home. Meaning, my only home, because I have never known another since.

I can see now the glistening meadows – meadows full of

snowdrops, marsh marigolds and buttercups, under constant threat from the rising Danube. And I can see the majestic hind-quarters of Grandfather's cows, and the round-shaped apple trees in the orchard. When the trees blossomed they looked like pink clouds, and the clouds in the sky – round puffy clouds – looked like blossoming trees. Above and below, there was no difference. Sometimes I imagine I can taste the taste of fresh bread on my tongue, or that of the yellow butter you can no longer get, now that all cows are milked mechanically. Everything we eat has lost its flavour. Chicken, pork and veal taste like soggy dishcloths. Last time I made a veal stew Hubert said, 'Ugh, where the devil is that smell of corpses coming from?' So, recently I've taken to using only beef, in the hope that adult cattle are more stubborn and refuse to eat anything other than grass and hay. Probably a good thing that Hubert smokes, and doesn't notice so clearly how foul everything tastes. It escapes him completely that the whipped cream stinks and the fish reeks of petroleum. Everything becomes more expensive but tastes nastier and nastier, and comes in more and more elaborate packages to make up for it. Only think what they have done to peaches: very soon you won't be able to eat them at all. Not to speak of sausages. I'd give everything we own for a good old fashioned slice of bread and butter.

The worst thing about this whole situation is that everyone knows it and hardly anyone talks about it. We uncomplainingly swallow down whatever is put before us. We are like oxen, plodding meekly along the beaten track with rings in our noses. On Saturday I bought preserved corn on the cob and artichokes. They were wildly expensive, and both tasted like pickled gherkins. Nobody seems to be responsible for this state of affairs, there is nobody to lay the blame on: from Minister to simple householder we all of us patiently consume the same brine-soaked blotting paper.

The fresh walnuts of my childhood came into my mind. When you rubbed together walnut leaves in your hand they released so strong a fragrance that it has left behind an indelible trace in my nose. Perhaps walnut leaves still smell like that today, but I don't dare go any deeper into the matter or put it to the test.

Or is it only me? Is it only inside me that things have changed? Is that what happens when you get older? I am forty seven, Hubert is fifty two; it could go on like this for quite a while yet. The days getting shorter and shorter, and the nights longer and longer, as we wake up and lie there, unable to sleep. This lying awake at night is slowly wearing us down. I notice straight away when Hubert is awake: he breathes differently, lighter, almost stealthily. Most likely I do the same. Both of us alone, thinking our own thoughts, and both hoping that the other partner in the next bed will not catch us out.

What goes on inside us during these nights, as we lie there on our backs, drifting downstream through time and listening for the far-off roar of the mighty waterfall that one day is going to engulf us? We know that miracles don't happen, that no one to date has ever escaped the waterfall, and that we are separated from those who have already reached it by only a tiny little span of time. One day – three years, ten years, twenty years. Sometimes it doesn't seem so terrible. I need to make no effort, don't even need to move my hands in the black water; it carries me along with it of its own accord. A gentle dizziness comes over me, and I know for certain: this one goal I will reach, even if I should fail all others. Probably because it is a goal I never set myself.

And far behind us, yet at the same time very close, at a distance we measure in years but that has nothing to do with years, our children drift along in the same direction. Only they don't know it yet, so their nights are short and deep and oblivious.

When I was still very young, sometimes, in broad daylight, the fear of death would sweep over me and I could feel my hair standing on end. The thought of not being there any more used to horrify me. Nowadays in the daytime I hardly ever think of it, and when I do I feel no fear. For that, there are the nights. Perhaps that is why Hubert never wants to go to bed. I still go to bed very willingly and go to sleep straight away – I have no problem on that account, it is simply that at four in the morning I wake up and am aware that slowly and sluggishly the current is carrying me forward. The roar of the great waterfall is hardly discernible, but there is no doubting that it is there, waiting for me.

I went on sitting at the table, and stared at my hands. My hands are older than my face, I find that very odd. It might have been some time since Ferdinand had left; it might only have been ten minutes. This kind of uncontrolled, free-wheel thinking, which is not real thinking at all, is recently becoming something of a habit. No, it's definitely not real thinking, it doesn't happen consciously, things just drift their way through me as if I was made of air. Maybe it happens all the time to old people, as they sit there in their armchairs and you can't tell whether they are asleep or awake.

But then, *are* there still old people in armchairs? The old people I see edge their way gingerly through the streets like crabs, one step forward, two steps back. They stand patiently at cash desks in shops, waiting for their turn, thinking how easy life was before self-service was introduced. They hobble up to the third floor in houses without lifts, heaving themselves tiredly on the banisters, and try to make ends meet on their scant pensions. They complain to one another about sciatica, varicose veins, asthma, heart trouble and water on the knee. On the streets they are fearful as hares pursued by hounds: unless they move fast enough, they've had it. And nobody wants them either – not the daughters, still less the sons. Life is short and grows daily shorter, and no one wants to be surrounded by ruins, unlovely in their decay.

Absentmindedly I put a piece of nut-roll in my mouth and nearly choked on it. The coughing fit brought me back to my senses. What point was there in thinking about old people whom I couldn't help and didn't particularly want to? Stands to reason I don't want to help them, I'm glad there are no old people left in my family. We are the old ones now, or at least the old*er* ones.

For some inexplicable reason, after the lift that Ferdinand's visit had given them, my spirits had sunk again, and were now at ground level. When that happens I daren't start giving in or feeling sorry for myself: there's only one remedy, I must deal myself a good kick. To date it has always worked. I must show no mercy, set myself the most unappetizing task I can think of and knuckle straight down to it. Kicks and a box on the ears are the best medicines for me: it must have something to do with my peasant ancestry. What other people do in similar circumstances, I don't know, and it's no business of mine anyway.

The bookshelves were the first thing that came to mind – it was six months since anyone had gone over them or dusted them. My sensitive side recoiled at the thought, but I wanted none of its moaning and groaning, so up I got from the table, found that one of my feet had meanwhile gone to sleep and stamped on it hard three times – stamping always helps bring back my courage. Of course, a visit to the dentist might work equally well, but I'd had a check-up only two weeks ago, and my dentist might be surprised to see me back so soon. Apart from which, the poor man was overworked and almost certainly suffered from lumbago and flat feet. When you consider it properly, dentistry is a frightful profession, much worse than others.

But now was not the time for considering anything: the bookshelves were waiting, and unless I was to go back on my resolve I must set to work immediately. I tied on an apron, bound my hair in a cloth and went and fetched the stepladder from the box room. One of the nicest things about this house is that it has still got a box room; it dates from a time when houses were built for people actually to live in.

I climbed onto the ladder, filled my apron with books, then climbed down again and took them out onto the veranda and stacked them on the table there. Then I started on them with duster and brush. I was amazed at the zest for work that suddenly came over me. I must have got it from my mother's side of the family because from what I know of my father he was restless and thirsty for life, but no great worker. As far as I remember (I was only eight when he died), what he liked best was playing cards, flirting with pretty young women, and sauntering around the main square of our little town of a Sunday. He was a bank employee and died of tuberculosis when he was thirty-eight. Maybe he wasn't really lazy by nature, just tired from all the poison in his body. I can remember him very clearly. He had a small face, dark hair, and green eyes that were set slightly aslant, and that were full of fun, especially when he felt well. I didn't particularly like him, not then. It was on his account that my mother never had time for me. I realised very early on that I was unwanted and superfluous, and that my mother had never desired anyone else apart from this handsome, sickly, unindustrious man who went through all her money with a flick of his delicate fingers. I was merely a side effect they had omitted to avoid.

Sometimes I was frightened of my mother. She was a great rosy, bright, blonde mountain. And like a mountain she towered over my father. She waited on him like a slave, but that didn't lessen the threat of her presence. I don't think he liked being waited on to such an extent but he couldn't defend himself. What she would have liked best was to have eaten him up and brought him to safety that way. After his death she was still a mountain, but a dead mountain; still blond and rosy, but aimless and indifferent to everything.

Even then she didn't need me. She didn't need anybody any more; all she needed was to get through the next few years somehow until she reached the point where she, too, was able to die. The disease was quite advanced in her already, of course: she had caught it from my father. I don't know whether I liked her either, although I probably did, since I can remember how much I minded her never letting me get into her bed. She smelt so nice, and she was so warm and soft, but she never let me into her bed. Nor would she have ever dared to – both my parents were very scrupulous about that, they didn't want to let me into their lives, still less into their deaths. I was never kissed by my parents, and my mother washed her hands continually. It could have been her way of loving me, but it could also have been a plain sense of duty.

I understood nothing of all this: I had cold toes and I wanted to warm them, in bed with my mother. She gave me a hot water bottle, which indeed warmed my toes, but the inner coldness remained.

Once, my father gave me a coral necklace: I was crazy about everything red. The necklace was a prickly thing and I later mislaid it. I was about six at the time, and my father was already very ill. He washed both the necklace and his hands before clasping it round my neck, so it felt cold and damp and made me shiver. I could tell he would have liked to pick me up and kiss me: his green eyes had a hungry look. To me it felt as if some unknown thing wanted to clutch hold of me and keep me, and I ran away. I don't recall what he said, my memory doesn't register voices, only pictures, but this picture I have is still very clear before my eyes. As I said, I lost the necklace later on. I always had a tendency to lose things – people too; it happened easily, like playing a game.

All this while I was climbing up and down the stepladder, my apron full of books, and I could feel a slight ache in my back. We have too many books. No one will ever read them. The only person who did perhaps read them was the elder Ferdinand. His books are bound in leather, some of them, and are valuable, but they are also badly yellowed and dusty. Hubert has never read any of them, apart from a world history in ten volumes and the ones about art and old battles. And, of course, the law books, but I don't really count those as books. I think Ferdinand senior read such a lot so as not to have to talk to his wife: in those days a man's authority was such that no one dared enter his study uninvited. And it was in this way that my dear father in law became so erudite.

I am very sorry that he had to die so soon, I would have liked to have known him better. His wife was vain and sly and cold: you'd never have warmed your toes on her. But she was definitely pretty, except for the starkness of her face. As a child she had acted in a pantomime, she had played the part of Snow White.

There was a picture of her in costume: a ten year old girl with long black plaits, a mocking smile on her small, heart-shaped mouth, her eyebrows arched into two thin black bows. A little stark, blank face. The elder Ferdinand must have fallen for this mask. It is a bit disturbing to think that Hubert takes after the mask more than he does his father – only in the mouth does he resemble Ferdinand, which is already a lot to be thankful for – but his face, too, is slightly stark.

And yet I wanted Hubert the moment I set eyes on him. He was not the first man in my life, but when I met him I forgot on the instant everyone and everything that had gone before. Hubert was never a stranger to me; he was familiar, as if we had known each other from childhood. He looked like a child, too – one who's never been allowed to warm his toes in his mother's bed. I didn't know that then, of course, but I reckon that must have been the basis of our closeness.

When I'm working hard, shinning up and down a ladder with my mouth full of bitter book-dust, I can't keep my thoughts under control. They run all over the place. In fact they do that all the time, even when I'm not working, but then I can keep better check on them.

Now my hands were completely black, and the bitter taste in my mouth was really incredible. Nothing is so bitter as the dust from old books. And there were still so many of them left. When they're set out in orderly rows you hardly notice them, but the moment you start taking them down they turn into a mountain you can barely see over.

I found myself holding a book that had belonged to my grandfather, a book about hunting, with those old fashioned illustrations in which the animals look quite different from what they do in real life. My grandfather didn't own many books – roughly thirty or so, I would say – but he read them his whole life long and knew them all practically by heart, his memory was so good. He used to read bits to me out loud without turning over the pages, and as a child I thought that was wonderful, a kind of magic. I don't know what happened to the other books; the only one I still had in my possession was the one with the weird animals. When it rained, and the Danube broke its banks, my grandfather used to sit in the parlour and read. When the waters went down again they left little puddles on the meadows, and the sky would mirror itself in these. I've never since seen such blue puddles. Blue was a very significant colour for me in those days, I loved blue. My mother's eyes were a true blue too; mine are greeny grey and slightly slanting like my father's were. But his eyes were fringed with thick, dark eyelashes. I have a feeling it was with those eyes that he lured my mother out of the big, wide house, and away from the puddles and the meadows and the green and white snowdrops.

My grandfather was unlucky with his family. His wife died young, and their only son was lamed by an accident in the sawmill. He was a big, handsome man, this son, but he never really came to terms with his handicap, and he married a woman who took him only for his money. They had a son who went missing in the war. My grandfather felt the loss hard, started to let things slide, and was never the same again. He had lost his two daughters already – my mother to Death and her sister to the cloister, which for him was much the same thing. He wasn't angry with her on this account, but he never mentioned her again. And his brothers died before he did – big strong men, all younger than he. They had married into the milling and timber trades, so in his heyday my grandfather was something of clan chieftain whom everyone came to for advice. His brothers had daughters only, one to each: they gravitated towards the families they married into. I barely knew them at all. In the end there was only me left, and my lame uncle who always sat next to the stove and drank too much because his leg hurt. Maybe he drank for other reasons too, but if so, nobody blamed him. He counted for little: his wife had taken the reins into her own hands and behaved as if he wasn't there.

My grandfather would willingly have left me all he possessed, but that was obviously impossible. Nor would I have wanted it: a lame son is still a son, and that my grandfather understood full well. He knew that everything would end up in strangers' hands, but he was already an ill man and past caring. It took him only three days to die; he recognised no one any more, not even me. But I sat with him alone for hours all the same and held his hand, and I've always been glad I did so: even if he couldn't see or hear any more, it's still possible he noticed that someone was holding his hand. You can't rule it out. I was left a little money that he'd set especially aside for me, and I moved to the city and enrolled in art school.

The only bad thing about this was that with his death I had lost the one place on earth where I felt truly at home. Much later on I learnt, quite by chance, that my lame uncle had died and his widow had married a forestry official. He was a good deal younger than she was and lived a flash life; her property, sawmill included, came under the auctioneer's hammer, and the capital was squandered. So in the end everything melted away – the broad-beamed house, the fields and meadows, the great, glossy cows and the fragrant woodpiles, the round apple trees, and everything I held dear.

The money was worthless, but that was not what mattered. I've never been back to Rautersdorf again. Strictly speaking, not even a stone of it belonged to me, but in my imagination I have always looked on it as my home.

I'd come to the classics now, and they seemed to go on for ever. Gold tooled covers and the print far too small, but none of us would read them, even if they were printed large. They tortured us with them at school and put us off them for good. They are all blurred in my memory – only a few insignificant fragments here and there remain. I always notice insignificant things and forget the important ones. For instance, of my mother's funeral all I remember is that it was very hot – a day in June with burning heat coming out of a white sky. The organ played off-key, and one of my great aunts (the ones by marriage whom I mentioned earlier) wore huge black shoes dusted over with graveyard earth. All the time I couldn't help thinking she was a man dressed as a woman, and the thought was so appalling that I began to cry. Quite why it was so appalling, I don't remember, but I do remember clearly envisioning the hairy masculine legs under the taffeta skirt. Those are the sort of things I notice, never the ones that are central to what's going on. And I'm still afraid of people dressed up as something they aren't, and a fancy dress ball is to me a nightmare.

Anyway, the classics were particularly dirty and I had to use the brush on them, raising, as I did so, a cloud of dust. It was cold on the veranda, and that suited me fine. I could, of course, have worn rubber gloves, but I couldn't bring myself to – I don't like wearing gloves of any kind. In winter, when I have to wear them, my fingers feel imprisoned and slightly numb.

My grandfather never wore gloves, and his hands were warm and dry and a nice browny red colour, even in deepest winter. For a long time I fancied I took after him, but that was only wishful thinking. In reality I am much more like my father. Only his tuberculosis I missed out on, but probably that was thanks to all the butter and milk and honey that I was fattened on in Rautersdorf. There were a lot of beehives there, and there was always a friendly humming sound in the air. When they worked in the fields the women looked rather like bees themselves – roundish and with blond hairs on their arms and legs and down the napes of their necks. I think their whole bodies may have been covered with this soft, downy fuzz. The men looked liked bumblebees, in their baggy brown trousers, and their voices were deep and purring. There were a number of hornets among them – big and flashy and dangerous, and forever chasing after the blonde bee-women.

Up the ladder again with the dusted classics. I'd made a lot of headway with my work; I must have looked like a chimney sweep, and I was so tired that if I'd stopped to rest I don't think I'd have been able to stand up again. You must never sit down when you're doing housework, not even for a second, because that's when tiredness jumps out and hits you. Now it was the turn of the travel books and biographies. Hubert has everything classified under categories, and I didn't dare mix them up. They weren't as grubby as the classics because they get read now and again, and they're on lower shelves, so I am able to dust them fairly regularly. It occurred to me that I might get a good night's sleep tonight, but I couldn't be sure. Hubert was dining with a client and was due back later than usual; there was nothing on TV that I needed to watch; therefore I could go up to the loft. In fact I *must* go up to the loft and confront the skeleton in my drawer. All this time I'd succeeded in suppressing this thought. I am good at suppression, out of long practise; had I not mastered the art my life would have turned to chaos. I have married a bourgeois man, run a bourgeois household and must behave accordingly. An evening in the loft is quite enough for me in the dissipation line.

The thought of the loft, however, repressed or not, made me uncomfortable, and I noticed that my hands were shaking. Could it be from the exertion of all the book clapping? Yes, I decided this was most probably the case. Suddenly I wasn't tired any more, and I stepped up the pace of my work. I could easily have cleaned out a second set of bookshelves but there was none there to clean. I knew only too well that up in the loft there was a piece of my past I had to liquidate. Actually it didn't feel as if the piece in question belonged to me in the least, but all bits of the past are best liquidated: it is a painful process that I've shirked from all my life.

A good thing that Hubert wouldn't be back till it was over. A relief, too, not to have to watch television.

Ilse hardly ever sits with us in the evenings. I find that a good thing too – that she leads her own life, I mean, and isn't hooked on viewing. She listens to music in her room, or studies, or goes out with friends. She has to be back by ten, and someone always has to accompany her – Hubert is very strict about this. Sometimes, but only very rarely, Ferdinand spends an evening with us; then Ilse comes out of her burrow and we all sit together and drink a bottle of wine. Ferdinand entertains us with stories that are probably all invented – much of what he says cannot possibly be true – but he's so good at talking about absolutely nothing, that you could hug him from sheer gratitude. In these moments we act as if we were a proper family, which is comical and tragic together. We wouldn't be able to keep it up for long, but since it happens so seldom it is a joy.

Dear Ferdinand – the child who cannot remember the real times we spent together. Once, an eternity ago, I made him a green frog out of an old waistcoat of his father's. It always had to go bed with him – dark green fabric pressed against sunburnt cheek. When I left I said to him, 'Be good, my love, I'll come back soon and bring you something special.' I was careful to speak quietly because I didn't know what my voice sounded like: I was stone deaf, you see, and was always terrified of shouting or croaking. Ferdinand smiled at me, and I saw his lips part. He said something, but I shall never know what it was.

When I came back, eighteen months later, the frog had disappeared. Almost certainly Madam Magistrate's doing: she was a great one for hygiene. Ferdinand didn't have anything left that he could have taken to bed with him, but he used to twist the corner of his pillow into a kind of doll and talk to that until he fell asleep. He had found a way of helping himself. The corner of the pillow wasn't that much more hygienic than the frog, but Madam Magistrate could do nothing about removing it. He didn't give up this habit until he was seven.

Ilse had fluffy animals and dolls from the start, but none of them was made by me. She didn't really need these things, either, as she was one of those children who fall asleep straight away. Occasionally she sucked her thumb, but only very rarely. Raising Ilse was a picnic. Maybe she was so easy because I never oppressed her with too much love and care. She got the exact amount she herself wanted, not a gram more. We have the same understanding today: she never, for instance, comes up to the loft to spy on me. I would never have managed that, I would always have followed my mother around, everywhere she went. But with my mother there was nothing to spy on, and nothing to rebel against either: she was there solely for my father, and after his death she was only a robot who went about her work and now and again succumbed to a fit of coughing.

Today I sometimes wonder whether my father did perhaps love me. I see those hungry green eyes of his, and I think to myself: maybe he would have liked to cuddle and kiss me, being by nature a tender and demonstrative man, but he couldn't do so because he couldn't allow his tenderness any expression. Maybe he reckoned it was already enough to have killed my mother that way. It takes a lot of self-discipline not to cuddle or kiss your own child. So today, when I look back on things, I feel sorry that all he was for me then was a nuisance – a cruel barrier separating me from my mother.

I was really pleased when he died and didn't have to cough any more at night. It was horrible – that barking, rasping cough that dragged me out of my childhood sleep – and I will never forget it. Sometimes I would cry out in fright, and then my mother would get very angry with me and say, 'Don't be so silly, it's just your poor father, gasping for air.' In daytime I could believe her, but by night it was all different. It was no longer my poor father, struggling for air, but a strange, horrifying creature that was being murdered in my parents' bedroom. I lay there in my bed, wet with sweat and shivering, and pulled the covers over my head, but the strange creature still went on crying out for help, and I was quite alone and at its mercy. Nobody comforted me then, because my mother truly didn't have the time; in fact, in these moments, I think she probably forgot I existed.

I understand all this now and don't hold it against her. It would be too late anyway. But that I couldn't show my anger at the time was bad for me, I think. I missed out on something important: a child must sometimes be able to hate its parents. As a result I could never quarrel with Hubert either. Sometimes I still try to, even today, but nothing ever comes of it – my anger just sounds funny and put-on. Hubert knows that perfectly well and smiles: he likes things this way, he quarrelled far too much with his mother, he prefers his women to be sweet natured. Maybe that was the reason he married me – a young man, tired of the endless fighting, who was looking for someone like me to afford him a rest. Can you tell that in a girl, I wonder: that she is unable to quarrel?

Ferdinand worries me – he is far too peace-loving. He doesn't give in, exactly; he merely wriggles out of things politely and firmly and does what he wants. But it would have been good for Hubert to have a son who stood up to him occasionally. Deep down he minds about this, but there's nothing he can do to change it. Sometimes I needle Ilse slightly, and she reacts normally and shouts at me and is even a bit rude. That pleases me, and I have to stop myself from congratulating her. Shout away, daughter of mine, I think to myself, defend yourself when you are attacked; with our anodyne friendliness we are trying to kill you, and this must not happen. Hubert doesn't like these scraps of ours. He is an aesthete, and it's ugly to see women fighting. Mind you, it doesn't happen often, I can't rouse myself that far as a rule, and even when I do, my anger doesn't last; I'm just no good at that sort of thing and Ilse knows it. Yes, it's a sort of lukewarm affair. I'm evidently not cut out for bringing up children. What I *am* cut out for, I don't really know either, seeing that in the paintings and drawings I do in the loft I never achieve my end.

One thing you can say of me, though, and that is that I try hard and don't give up easily. Once in a while I even dust the book-shelves. I never grumble, and I don't get too much on my family's nerves. At least I hope I don't – you never can be quite sure. Because if I don't, then why did Ferdinand move out? A less sensitive son might have simply said, 'I've had enough of you lot, I'm going my own way now. This life of yours bores me stiff, it's no real life at all, it gives me the creeps. I'm off!' The fact that he didn't say it is no proof that he didn't think it. We don't know what Ferdinand thinks, and that's probably the most humane solution for all three of us.

By seven o'clock I'd finished with the bookshelves. I lay in the bath and let the dirt float off me in streams. That's the sort of thing a man never thinks about: that his books are covered with dust and that every so often some woman must come and remove it. What would a man do, who had no wife and no paid cleaner, but a huge library? I can't imagine. What do men think anyway about what happens to all the dirt that accumulates around them? They probably don't think about it all, or only in an abstract way. Roughly like this: Time Mrs So and So came and tidied this place up a bit. And while this man is sitting in his nice clean office (clean, because another Mrs So and So has just been over it), back at home the first Mrs So and So is bustling around in her struggle against dirt and dust. And when the man gets home everything is clean again, and it doesn't surprise him one little bit because he has no idea of what's been going on behind his back. He gets into his freshly made bed, and next morning he puts on a white shirt that a third Mrs So and So has washed and ironed for him, and leaves the house under the illusion that the world is a clean and orderly place. The only rubbish that he has to clear away himself is the growth of his own beard, and he groans about it in front of the mirror and leaves the bathroom in a state that wrings a groan from Mrs So and So as well; and when he gets back again in the evening, he is still quite unfazed to find everything back in order. And those unfortunates who have no Mrs So and So? They raise untidiness to the level of a virtue, and grow beards so as to sidestep even that one little chore.

While I was making these admittedly rather biased considerations, my tiredness had disappeared. I could have kidded myself my hot bath had been a cold shower, were it not for the fact that I'm no hero and can't abide cold water. I don't believe anyone takes cold showers, not really, but if they do, then they can't be normal; they must be throwbacks to another species, maybe an amphibious one that died out in prehistoric times from the very habit of taking cold baths.

I towelled myself dry, gave my hair a quick blow with the blow-drier, and slipped on a dressing gown. A cup of tea might have done me good, but I couldn't spare the time: I had spent so many years already putting off the unpleasant task of revisiting the past, I couldn't afford to lose a minute more. I went straight upstairs to the loft, paid no attention to the tempting pens and pencils but took the envelope out of the drawer, pulled out the yellowing pages that lay inside and began to read.

Pruschen, September 6th

I don't like the gamekeeper. He looks at me as if he wondering whether for Hubert's family's sake he oughtn't to shoot me dead. He's used to giving sick animals the *coup de grâce*. I'm hiding these papers in the mattress because it's unlikely anyone will look for them there. Not that it would matter much if the gamekeeper came across them; I doubt he could even read my handwriting.

He wouldn't want to read them either, I'm not interesting in any way, not half as interesting as a cripple would be. You can live with a cripple because you can talk to a cripple. If I were repulsively ugly, for instance, or had a hump or a huge red birthmark, then people could be sorry for me or make fun of me; but they can't do that because I can't hear their pity, or their mockery either. I must seem weird to them, and my company hard to endure.

But I still wouldn't like the gamekeeper, even if I was a proper able-bodied person again. In his eyes – those eyes that have no colour to them at all – I can see nothing except calculation. He is greedy and treats his animals rough. I can tell that because I can see it: I'm deaf all right but I'm not blind. He's rough to them, not out of anger but because he despises them and they depend on him. I'm on a lower level still than they are, but he is paid to take me in and, up to a certain point, to take care of me. He probably finds me just about as useful as his cow, the only difference being that the cow turns her head towards him when he shouts at her. The fact that he daren't quite treat me like the cow infuriates him. Sometimes he seems to be frightened of me – maybe on account of some superstition or other. There's no telling what goes on inside that head. If he weren't so avid for the money he would never have taken me in. I don't think he feels any gratitude now towards my father in law, to whom he owes so much. The old man is dead and of no use to him any more. Maybe he wants to impress the village with his loyalty to his one-time patron. But again, maybe not. The people here have known him since he was born, and they can see through his actions as clearly as he through theirs. Gamekeepers are often unpopular: they are still looked on as lackey-figures who don't quite belong in the village and whom nobody can really trust.

September 12th

My room is small, with tiny windows, and it's rather dark because the house is set right against the slope of the mountain. Anyone could easily climb up to me by shinning up a tree outside, but the windows are barred, giving the room a prison-like aspect. The gamekeeper's house is somewhat brighter because the windows look out onto the valley side. He gets the morning sun, and I would get the midday sun if the mountain didn't lie between me and the light. There are far too many mountains here. I've never liked mountains much.

My father in law used to sleep in this room when he was here for the hunting season. I don't think he was that keen on hunting really, he just wanted to get away from his wife. The furniture belonged to him, and the gamekeeper has inherited it. A rustic bedstead with a painted headboard – God's eye looking out at me from it, whether I'm asleep or awake. Then there's a painted chest, a small writing table and an old brown leather armchair that you can curl up in and almost disappear. In the corner stands a green-tiled stove, and close by it a little kitchen with a built-in range, a wobbly cupboard and a simple stripped-pine table. At the far end of the kitchen lies the bathroom: my father in law had it specially put in to save himself the bother of going downstairs. I don't use the range; I cook on an electric ring. The gamekeeper doesn't approve of this: he glares in rage at such extravagance, but he's paid so much money that he daren't criticize openly. The gamekeeper isn't young any more but he isn't old either; he still carries out all his duties. He's away a lot during the day, but he has to be home mornings and evenings in order to milk his cow. Either he never had a wife or she died; I tend to think the latter, that he is a widower.

The door of my bedroom leads onto a wooden balcony, from which a flight of stairs takes you down to ground level. This makes me very happy – as happy as I can be under the circumstances. In the mornings I sometimes sit on this balcony in search of a little sunlight. I sit on a very hard chair with a heart carved in its backrest. When I stand up again my head bumps against a pair of antlers – the veranda is hung all over with bleached bones.

The sun comes latish, never before nine o'clock: it has to climb over the mountains opposite first. In front of the house runs a little trout stream called the Prush; at present it has very little water because it's so long since it last rained. On the far bank of the Prush the mountain already begins to soar. I sit here as if in a cage. Behind the mountains lie little valleys, or so I imagine, and then more and more mountains.

My grandfather had a big, spacious house; round it lay pastures that the cows used to graze on – proper big cows, nothing like the poor creature that belongs to the gamekeeper. All day long you could see the sun, and you felt free there, and safe. If my grandfather were still alive he would have had me stay with him, and I wouldn't be alone: it wouldn't have bothered him that we couldn't talk to one another, we never talked much anyway. But he is dead and cannot help me. Nobody can help me. I don't give much thought to Hubert or little Ferdinand – it's not a good idea to think about them much.

I sit huddled up in the leather armchair, using my knees as a writing table. I've felt tired ever since I got here. But I don't want to write the place off too soon: maybe the silence and fresh air will be good for me. And it's not as if anywhere else in the world wouldn't be just as silent. So maybe it's the air, then, that's making me so tired: I reckon I'll have to get accustomed to it.

November 1st

The gamekeeper has gone off to the cemetery with a big bunch of fir twigs and Michelmas daisies. His dog went with him. I don't quite know whether I like this dog or not: he's old and ugly, and I feel sorry for him because he has the gamekeeper for a master.

Hubert has written to say he's coming soon to visit me. He writes me a letter every Sunday: he's a very methodical and orderly person. It's kind of him, though, when you think how much work he has, even if he doesn't say much in his letters. He's given up the apartment we rented and has moved in with his mother. A good thing really because I don't like to think of little Ferdinand being brought up by his grandmother alone. Of course, there's Serafine the cook as well, but she's just the old woman's slave and doesn't count for much. When Hubert has built a life for himself he'll look for another apartment and come and fetch me back. Provided I pull through, that is, and am able to hear again. The doctors have told him there's nothing physically wrong with me; it's just that I've forgotten how to hear. Hopefully I'll remember again. Meanwhile I sit here, and that's best for all concerned. Ferdinand is getting on fine, Hubert writes. Which means he's forgotten about me, because otherwise how could he be fine? A three year old child forgets quickly. He's already been six months with my mother in law. A deaf mother wouldn't really be good for him at all.

I think I'll write to Hubert and tell him not to come: it would only distress us both unnecessarily. Better for him to concentrate on his work and on the new life he has to create. I know Hubert well: he won't be able to build a new life and think of his deaf wife at the same time, it would utterly confuse him. After our little world fell apart he finally took a grip on himself and tried to put things in some sort of order: he's a great one for putting things in order. I am to try to get well and calm my nerves so that I can remember how to hear

47

again. Ferdinand will be brought up and taken care of by his grandmother, and Hubert will rebuild a life. And if we all pull our weight and do our duty, everything will be well again, and we can once more live together, and everything will be as it was before.

It's possible that Hubert truly doesn't realise that nothing will ever again be the way it was before. I'm younger than him, and yet I know it – presumably because it's already happened to me to lose everything I had. A dead grandfather doesn't come back to life again, and neither do dead parents, I have known that for a long time. You can't even stitch a broken doll together without it looking different from what it originally was. But I'm glad for Hubert that he hasn't learnt this yet; and anyway, it won't be long before he does.

November 13th

It still hasn't rained. The weather has recently become very important to me; I never really used to notice it before. But here there's nothing except the weather, it offers the only opportunity for change. Since yesterday night it has been hot and muggy with a strong wind blowing from the south. I can't hear it, but I can see the trees swaying and the bushes waving around in silent uproar. High winds always unsettle me, especially when they come from the north, but the south wind doesn't affect me so much. I see the branches whipping against the roof; now and again one of them brushes across my window. And since the windows don't shut properly I can also feel the draught: it touches my face and lifts the hair from my forehead. I crawl deeper into the leather armchair. It's hard to write in this position; I think I'll read a bit instead.

The gamekeeper has a weird habit: he writes me terse little notes. 'Anything I can bring you from the village?' 'Got to go and fetch more wood.' For these notes he uses torn off calendar leaves; he scribbles them right under my nose, and then, instead of handing them over, he tears them into tiny pieces and shoves them in the stove. He always waits until they are completely burned – each time he destroys the evidence. I bet he'd be furious if I took one of these notes from him, although I can only tell this from his eyes: the rest of his face is totally expressionless. A wan, flaccid face with grey beard-stubble. He doesn't look as if he was outdoors all day. His face reminds me of a half-done wood carving that no one has taken the trouble to finish. But, then, what point would there be in taking a note from him and making him angry? I depend on him completely; he brings in the wood for me and does all my shopping. Of course, I could do these things for myself, and one day I hope I shall. It's all wrong that I can't bring myself to go into the village and hand my shopping list to the lady behind the counter on my own account, but the mere thought of it makes my hands go cold and clammy. What could happen if I did? Nothing at all. The village people are bound to know all about me already. The worst they could do is stare, but I'm used to that by now. Except, no, that's not true, I haven't got used to it or I wouldn't be here. Looking back over the past six months, I'm glad Hubert brought me to this place. The gamekeeper doesn't care one way or the other: he'd hide a murderer if he was paid enough, and who knows that he hasn't already done so. At least you can talk to a murderer, and there are probably some pretty affable and entertaining murderers around.

Today it occurred to me that I never ask myself why this thing should have happened to me of all people. It would have been such an obvious question to ask. I suspect it is because secretly I have known all along that our happiness could not last. I didn't know it consciously, of course, but that is the way it must have been. And yet I was a very ordinary child and sometimes I was downright happy. Why is it that this strange being inside me just doesn't want to hear? And why did it happen now – at a time when at last I had achieved what I had always wanted: a family of my own? Life was so good.

So here I sit, waiting until the strange being inside me decides to start hearing again. The doctor said it could happen tomorrow, or on the other hand might never happen at all. No one seemed to know much about it, so in the end I stopped going to doctors, I couldn't bear all the fuss.

It is dark now and the branches of the beech tree sway, black, outside the window. A gust of wind blows through the room. I intended to read, but instead I sit absolutely still and wait.

I stuffed the pages back in the envelope and went down to the cellar. There I put them in the burner and waited until they were completely burned. I was behaving like the gamekeeper and getting rid of the evidence. Not until there was no trace of them left, save for a layer of fine grey ash on the glowing coals, did I sit down on an empty beer crate and attempt to think. That far-off day I had put my papers in the suitcase, under a layer of clothes. When I had unpacked again, back in the new apartment, they were no longer there. I had reckoned I must have forgotten to pack them after all and had probably burned them instead by mistake on that last evening in Pruschen, together with some old newspapers and stuff. It was unlikely that the gamekeeper would have stolen them: they would have meant nothing to him, and besides, I hadn't yet told him that I was leaving. I could remember it clearly now: he wasn't home that day, he was out in the woods somewhere, or in the village, and I had been out in the woods again, too, and had got back before he did. My case was already packed by the time I went to arrange with him about my departure, and I didn't bother to check if I had packed everything or not. My room was never locked: anybody could have slipped in under the cover of darkness and taken the papers. But only one person came to mind. I had done my best to forget him and I had in fact succeeded: very soon afterwards I had stopped thinking about him altogether. Certain things and certain people I just cannot afford to think about if I want to go on living, and he was one of them. Why should he suddenly turn up again now, after so many years – an old man who was frightened of me because I knew too much?

It was so comical that I had to laugh. The laughter shook my whole body. For sixteen years, no matter where he had been during this time or what he had done, he had been frightened of me, and I had never given him a thought. His fear in itself was not so funny, but the fact that he had felt it (and was still feeling it) without any reason to do so was a total absurdity, but I could never explain this to him because he would never believe me. Anything that could happen now would come far too late and have no point to it at all.

I went up to the living room again. To my surprise Hubert was there, in front of the television, staring at the screen. His dinner date must have fallen through. On the table stood the crystal ashtray; it looked very heavy. I could easily have killed him with it, but I had no desire to do so. I might as well have killed myself with it for all the difference it would make today.

Hubert turned his head and smiled at me. 'You wouldn't get me a sandwich, would you,' he said, 'and a glass of beer?'

I went into the kitchen and cut him a couple of sandwiches, and carried them and the beer into the living room. Hubert looked very harmless: a middle aged man who goes to his office every day in order to feed and house his family. I noticed that his hair was getting thinner at the back, and that touched me deeply. He carries, on his none too broad shoulders, a load that is too heavy for him to bear, but he never complains. It was the least I could do for him, to bring him some sandwiches and glass of beer, and it was practically all I could do for him too.

The beer made him sleepy and he started yawning. This evening I didn't say to him, as I usually do: 'Why don't you go to bed?' He's dead tired every evening, but I know perfectly well he doesn't want to go to bed. So there we sat for another hour or so and listened to a debate in which six people, who appeared to know one another quite well, talked at and over and across each other without listening to a word anybody else said. I couldn't make out what it was they were talking about, but then I hardly ever can. I have the impression that recently a new language has been invented that I simply cannot understand. But on this evening my thoughts were somewhere else anyway, which was quite understandable. Finally, round about eleven, I took myself off to bed and went to sleep straight away. Later I noticed that the bed was moving under Hubert's weight and saw how his hand stretched out to stroke my shoulder. It could have been a dream, though; I often can't tell the difference.

Tuesday

At half past seven the alarm clock went off. I had lain awake from four until six and then fallen fast sleep. Five minutes before the alarm rang, though, I was already awake again. I always am. We don't really need an alarm but Hubert doesn't trust the clock in my head.

I hate that alarm. It sits on Hubert's bedside table so I can't reach it to switch it off. I am convinced this wretched thing is slowly killing us – a fraction every day. Merely waiting for it to start ringing is in itself a torment. The noise it makes frightens me. Hubert mistrusts me and has forbidden me to touch it: according to him I have already murdered two alarm clocks on the sly. This is not true; it's simply that they don't like being touched by me since they dislike me as much as I do them. Sometimes I dream up possible ways of maltreating them and this calms me down a bit. Hubert kids himself into believing that alarm clocks are innocuous instruments; in his unquestioning way he even thinks they are useful. But then he hasn't a clue what is good for him and what isn't. Hateful noisy machines, inventions of the devil! Before the day can slip noiselessly into the room it is shattered to pieces by this vulgar rattling noise. Mind you, it's difficult to do anything right by me, I realise this. Basically I don't like anything made of metal at all. There ought to be wooden alarm clocks that creak softly like old floorboards, or singing alarm clocks made of glass or stone that make a faint scrunching noise and release a trickle of sand. Anything but these hard shiny metal clocks. Oh, I grant, metal isn't really ugly, it possesses a smooth, vicious kind of beauty, but it's a beauty I don't admire. Plastic objects, on the other hand, I neither like nor dislike: they are simply ugly, and they're not even dead, they are just nothing.

The alarm rang, and today it was particularly shrill. A suitable start to a fourth Tuesday in the month – the day on which I have to go and see the Baroness.

Hubert sat up in bed and said, 'Good morning'. He says that every day. Nice manners are built into him, his mother saw to that. If only for once he were to say, 'Damn, time to go back to the treadmill,' it would make a wonderful change. It would mean that his stiff outside shell had broken and the real Hubert I used to know was visible again. But that will never be. He sat up straight and ran his fingers through his rumpled hair. Today it seemed to me greyer than usual. He is a man who either sleeps like a stone or is wide awake – half measures are unknown to him, which is why he doesn't like the twilight. He switched on the light, clambered out of bed and went into the bathroom.

I was very tired, and a crowd of loft-thoughts pressed about me. My head was still shattered by the noise of the alarm and I found it hard to defend myself against them. That's what happens when you drift downstream all night long and can't get off to sleep. To put an end to this I sprang out of bed and donned my dressing gown. The spring came out rather pathetic – my bones ached all over and reminded me of yesterday's bookshelf orgy.

Breakfast with us is a dull affair. Hubert only takes black coffee and a thin slice of wholemeal bread – a dismal sight for a person like me who enjoys a good breakfast. He doesn't even put sugar in his coffee. It's an army habit of his that I think it's time he gave up. It dampens my pleasure in honey and marmalade and freshly baked bread. Because I need something sweet in the mornings, particularly on a fourth Tuesday in the month when the Baroness looms before me.

Hubert reads the paper while he breakfasts. That's not so much a bad army habit as a bad male habit in general. For years he had to abstain from this vice since in his mother's house it was, naturally, frowned on. But I think he can afford to indulge in it now – a pinch of vice can only do him good. Besides, it means that I don't have to watch him at his frugal breakfast. He's grateful to me for letting him have his way over this matter of the newspaper. He doesn't say so, but I can tell it from the affectionate, guilty look he gives me. It's impossible to free him from these guilty feelings of his, partly because he's so used to having them, and partly because, like everyone else, he has grounds for them. His conscience, though, is that much stricter and harsher than most other people's, and against a conscience there's not really much that you can do.

After ten minutes he folded up the paper – he is very precise about things like that – bent over me and kissed me on the cheek with his cool, dry mouth and said, 'I'll be back about one. Have a good morning.'

'Bye,' I said, and then added softly, 'Drive carefully, won't you!'

To this he made no reply. He knows there's no dissuading me from pronouncing this childish magic formula. I know it myself: I do it out of sheer compulsion and it would be a waste of energy to try to resist. It's important to know what's possible and what isn't, and for me *not* to say, 'Drive carefully' is impossible. Hubert doesn't hear me any more and anyway it can't do any harm.

I stretched out for the paper and leafed through it. There was nothing of interest in it at all, not once you have grown accustomed to the fact that there is always a war on somewhere, and that children starve, and that in our own peaceful land every day a couple of people bleed to death in car accidents, and men kill their wives and women their husbands. There seem to be a lot of alcoholics around too, and a lot of mental cases. And on top of all this there are the natural catastrophes to be relied on: people constantly freezing to death in one spot of the globe and dying of thirst in another.

How friendly in comparison seem the reports of fraud and burglary. Downright refreshing almost. Every time I read a newspaper I feel really well disposed towards these people who go about their non-violent business and yet who are punished almost as severely as the murderers and manslaughterers. Money seems to be so incredibly important, you're not supposed to lay a finger on it, and I find this strange and hard to understand. But then what *don't* I find strange and hard to understand? I put the paper aside, not very carefully folded, and wished good luck for the day to all thieves, especially the petty ones.

Then I began to tidy up. The butter looked anaemic, and the cream was sterilized. I put both away in the fridge, and the vision of a yellow pat of butter appeared before my eyes. Then I saw a spring, in front of a house I must no longer let myself think about, and out of the spring ran clear, cold water with a trace of chlorine in it. I shook my head, slightly dazed, and felt a nagging hunger and thirst. Then I realised I had just had breakfast, and the strange feeling disappeared leaving nothing but sadness. It was much too early for sadness so I pushed it away, telling it it could come back in the evening, if it liked, in the loft, and it obeyed me immediately and went.

By nine I had finished the housework and went out to do the shopping. I have nothing against self service shops: I've never liked talking to the other shoppers much, I'm not a great one for talking. At the butcher's I had to wait a while and I heard the most amazing bits of conversation. It transpires that a lot of old people live in our district. They are all either suffering themselves or have bedridden relatives at home; at the butcher's you hear things you would normally hear in a doctor's waiting room. For all their woes, however, these women took their time about their shopping, and hardly any of them seemed to know what they wanted to buy. I pitied the poor butcher's boy – a big strapping young man who stood there and waited with exemplary patience. Now and again he rolled his eyes to the ceiling, leaving just the whites showing, but not a cross word escaped him, only an occasional little sigh. Several women didn't seem to make their minds up until their meat was wrapped, and then suddenly opted for a different cut altogether – it made for slow progress. Finally the group of woebegones moved on, chattering happily, to drive some other shopkeeper to distraction. Maybe they get some fun out of life this way. I hope they do, because if not my impatience with them would reach bursting point.

There was grey, mushy snow on the street – not much of it, but enough to slip on and for the cars to splash you with as they passed. The street is very wide at this point and there is no pedestrian crossing, so it is quite an undertaking to get to the other side. You often see old people hesitating for ages at the curb before they dare embark on the adventure. The sight reminds me of those big shooting parties where the wild animals are driven mercilessly by the beaters towards the guns. It is a wonder anyone manages to get across, but I manage it all right. Those who don't are either culled on the spot, or else end up in hospital or in a clinic for nervous disorders where the worst of the damage is repaired and the patients are sent out again to face another battery of guns. Even my strong old grandfather, the chieftain of his tribe, would cut the figure of a clumsy old country bumpkin were he here today, and wouldn't stand a chance of making it to the other side. I'm glad he never had to know about such things.

As I walked home (living in the outskirts, the trip takes me about ten minutes from the centre of town), I suddenly realized that I must erase the Baroness from my life completely. She was another person who belonged to the past, and since I was now engaged on wiping out the past, she too must go. I couldn't, obviously, shove her in the burner, but it would be sufficient simply not to visit her any more. This thought put me in a more cheerful mood. Did I really have to put up with her any longer, simply because once upon a time I used to lodge with her, and to let her cling to me in the air-raid shelter, her teeth chattering like castanets? No, that was not enough, I decided, to bind two human beings together for life. She wasn't the only one whose teeth had chattered, either; in those days everyone's teeth chattered, mine included. Especially during night raids. For some reason I couldn't bear the sirens. It wasn't the bombs I feared; it was the howling noise over the town. It was silly of me but that was the way it was. The sirens went on to persecute me in a later period too, and gave my life a most unwelcome twist, but that was my private affair and was no reason why I should endure the Baroness any longer.

In those days it would have been easy to break things off: easier to let a fifty year old down than a sixty year old. Although I don't know if this true in the Baroness's case. She is ageless. At fifty she was just as ghastly as she is today, and at sixty she is not a whit weaker or more helpless. Hatred keeps her healthy and happy. She's a born manslaughteress. It might be a good thing if she could actually deliver her deathly blow and then settle down peacefully to become an old woman, if a lonely one. But she has missed her opportunity. The one person she wanted to kill has meanwhile brought himself to safety. There is no way she can reach him in his grave in the municipal cemetery where he now resides. And anyway, even after a successful attempt she would never be a normal old woman, she would be far less, she would be nothing, and she prefers to be a fiend brimming with hatred than nothing. With people like that I just give in – which doesn't say much for my strength of character, I'm afraid.

I don't know how I got home. At some point I simply found myself there, washing Hubert's socks in the basin. It's weird how you can entertain thoughts in your head while nothing in the outside world changes at all. The mirror over the basin was slightly misted over by steam, and a couple of drops ran slowly down its silver-coated surface. It looked as if I was crying, but it was only the mirror crying because I never cry any more. The last time I did so was after I returned from Pruschen – in my first night back with Hubert. I thought then that all would be well again because I could still cry. And all might have been well if Hubert had cried with me. But he's a man, of course, and ever since he was a small boy he has been trained not to. If, of a couple, only one person cries, nothing good can come of it, there can be no real deliverance from evil. So I soon lost the habit of doing so. You have no idea how easy it is to lose: you tell yourself nothing's really altered, one day the occasion will arise and you'll cry again, but when the occasion presents itself you find you can no longer do it.

So now there was only the mirror to do my crying for me. That was a bit unnerving, and I lowered my eyes and kept them on the washing. I never feel humiliated by performing what are considered lowly jobs. Somebody's got to wash dirty socks, after all, there's no shame attached to it. And even if there were, I would still prefer the shame to dirty socks. The only annoying part about it is that while I wash things I can still think. When I paint or draw I don't think, or think only about the business in hand: how can I manage to draw a bird that is not the only bird in the world? True, this thought is only important to me, not to anyone else, but it's a thought I needn't be ashamed of – it's a nice straightforward thought that excludes all others. Whereas to wash socks with a hundred things buzzing around inside your head is a schizoid state of affairs and it makes me dithery and nervous.

How nice it would be just for once not to have to think at all; to be just a body in space, moving around deftly and freely. To know that time is merely a construct and that nothing forces me to hurry. I would like, just for once, to take a good look at things and see them the way they really are, and not the way they show themselves to us. That's why I like going to sleep, because in the moment of passage there's nothing in your head but images: no time, no thoughts, just images, and then lights out and total blankness. I usually go to sleep lying flat on my stomach, which is supposed to be a sign of a mean, self-centred character. And so I may be – mean and self-centred – but personally I find it a great privilege to be able to sleep on my front and turn my back on the world, for a couple of hours at least.

Tonight I would not get off to sleep so easily, that was already clear to me. Not on account of the loft-thoughts – I never take those to bed with me – but on account of the Baroness. She's not conducive to sleep, even though she tires me to the point of exhaustion. But on the other hand she would serve to take my mind off all those half-buried thoughts and fears that were pressing on me constantly, refusing to stay put in the loft where I had tried to leave them. The Baroness was at least a horror with which I was familiar, and better an old horror than a new, unknown one.

Hubert knows very little about the Baroness, he thinks she's just a harmless old acquaintance whom I visit out of charity. And even if he knew that wasn't so, he wouldn't offer an opinion. He's a rational man, by which I mean that he desperately would *like* to be rational. Reason is to him the most desirable quality in the world, he can think of nothing that beats it. I have a feeling this is because he is basically highly *ir*rational and doesn't dare admit it. A truly rational man would never have married me for a start. For four years he did in fact allow himself to be irrational, and he was the most lovable being I could ever have imagined. I wonder if he remembers. Probably not, or not clearly anyway, because everything we did then must seem to him today utter madness. No, I'm sure he has decided to forget it, the way I also have decided to forget certain things in my life – quite a number of things actually. You can manage to do this if you practise hard enough.

As I rinsed the socks out I realised I was very angry with Hubert. This always happens quite against my will. It is so unfair of me. Hubert had to re-make a life for himself. Where would we be today if he hadn't gone about it? He did exactly what needed doing and what he couldn't avoid doing. But it could have killed me. Although, mind you, that might have been no great loss: Hubert could have remarried – a proper grown-up woman this time, not a frightened child; Ferdinand would have had a nice, reasonable mother; and Ilse would never have been born. No, Ilse would never have been born, and that is difficult for me to imagine: she is so real and alive, and is made of milk and blood, and has my mother's eyes.

I could look at people's eyes for hours on end. You're not supposed to, of course, because it annoys their owners. My grandfather had very blue eyes – not that pale, cloudy blue you see in shifty characters of a certain type, but a deep, peaceful blue, which with time grew brighter and more translucent until, in the last weeks of his life, it became veiled over by a kind of whitish film. As happens to sick animals on the point of death. My eyes are a greenish blue-grey colour, just a trace of the true blue in them, but mostly that hungry green: eyes that want to devour everything they see.

When I say that Ilse has my mother's eyes that is not quite right, there's a touch of Hubert's grey in them too – a very staunch colour. Ilse would never marry a sick, decorative man and aspire to be his servant. No, Ilse, never, for sure – which is why I needn't worry about her.

Ferdinand has very peculiar eyes, dark and foreign, as if they came from a different world from ours. There's no reading eyes like that and they make me feel a little unsure.

But that's all nonsense really. Eyes are simply there for us to see with. I can't imagine anyone but myself troubling their heads about the colour of people's eyes. Sometimes, though, this idiosyncrasy of mine is a real torment: I can't go up to totally unknown people and ask them if I can stare into their eyes. You can never really, in any sphere, do what you want to do. But why not? I wouldn't be angry or surprised if someone wanted to look into my eyes. It's not done, that's why, and you have to bow to this. There are certain rules that just have to be followed, and to my mind they make life colourless and dull.

I stood up straight and pushed back the hair from my forehead. The mirror was streaming tears so I opened the window wide to enable it to stop its crying. No, the colour of things surely can't be wholly without importance. It must mean something. I thought of the jay's blue feathers and the yellowy grey plumage of starlings, and the way it shimmers when the sunlight catches it. There must be some meaning to all that, it's just that I can't fathom it.

And then there was that starling that I nearly got right. They say that starlings can talk together like people can. My starling looked as if it was listening to starling-talk from the next-door garden. That bird should not have gone missing. It was the beginning of something – something that I never achieved again. A lot of far more important things went missing during that time as well, but to me the starling *was* important: I was happy with it. I hung the socks on the washing line on the veranda and went into the kitchen. At last I was able to put the awkward loft-thoughts out of my mind and concentrate on cooking lunch. It was about time too; I'd been very undisciplined today. Then, the moment I started defreezing the spinach, a thought suddenly occurred to me that for a second left me numb. I ran outside to the gate and opened the letterbox. There was nothing inside save for another thick yellow envelope. I had know all along, of course, that there would be, and had deliberately avoided looking in the letterbox until now. But this time it didn't cause me any shock – there was no surprise, in a sense it was almost reassuring. I went up to the loft and put the thing into a drawer: in future it might come to seem quite normal to receive a yellow envelope every day. I lost no time but went straight back downstairs to my spinach again. I felt quite relieved: things were running their normal course. The spinach had nearly thawed out and I began melting some butter.

At one o'clock Hubert came home. He had nothing to do with the yellow envelope, not this Hubert, and the other Hubert was no longer there. Just as the strange young woman who had written those lines in a copy book was no longer there. There was no point allowing myself to get worked up about it, all this had nothing to do with me any more either. Hubert looked tired. I think he works too hard. This house costs a lot of money to run. It's old and things constantly need repairing. Basically the house is eating us up. We don't have expensive tastes, Ilse needs no more than other young girls her age, and Ferdinand only gets a substantial present now and then when it's his birthday or something. If he was still living with us Hubert would willingly work harder to pay for his keep; he resents the fact that this function has been taken away from him. I am the only one who is pleased about it; I like Ferdinand to feel free, or free enough, anyway, not to be aware all the time of the chains that bind him, which is already quite an achievement.

What happens to money, I wonder? It melts away and you never know how. Hubert keeps the accounts; I never ask what it has all gone on. It's his house and his money, and he must know what he's doing. He could talk to me about it if he liked, but apparently he doesn't want to. We take a holiday every year, and Hubert has a weakness for art books, so there evidently must be enough to cover those expenses. We are neither of us extravagant. Of course there's the car, but that we need. And there's also the fact that Hubert is no handyman: he has nice brown hands with thin fingers but he can't so much as hammer in a nail with them, so we are at the mercy of workmen. There's something not quite right about this, but I get the feeling it's best to close an eye and not to meddle: anything that would injure Hubert's self-esteem must be avoided. He wants to play the part of the all-round family man, and so he shall. I have the impression he is conserving the house for Ilse. He thinks it's unfair that Madam Magistrate left all her money to Ferdinand and not a penny to Ilse.

I don't agree with him, though. To me it was quite in order. If there was anyone who gave the old woman pleasure it was Ferdinand. He made her a present of two happy years as well – there's no amount of money that can pay for that.

Hubert sat down at the table and we ate in silence, neither of us concentrating much on what we were doing. The atmosphere was friendly enough, it was simply that we were both elsewhere in our thoughts. Hubert in particular: only his body was there, taking in the nourishment it needed. He could achieve the same purpose in a restaurant, naturally, but no, Hubert comes home to eat whenever he can because he prefers sitting in silence by my side to sitting in silence anywhere else. I suppose you could look on it as a declaration of love.

After the meal he went to lie down for twenty minutes. Twenty minutes exactly, during which time he slept soundly. Then he surfaced again, wide awake and looking less tired than before.

We drank some coffee and smoked a cigarette, and he told me he'd met So-and-so and So-and-so that morning. Names that meant nothing to me, but I acted as if I was really interested. Actually, I probably was quite interested: everything you hear is interesting in some way or another.

Soon after this he was ready to be off again. I reckon the reason he likes his work so much is because it prevents him from thinking about things he'd rather not think about. It's funny, he used to be rather delicate and suffered from endless coughs and colds, but with time he's lost this weakness of his. To me, it has something to do with the fact that he's slightly drying up all over – not enough moisture in him any more for catarrh or a runny nose. Every so often he has a slight attack of rheumatism, and I think his heart may give him a bit of worry. He says nothing to me about it but sometimes I catch an anxious look on his face, as if he were listening to something inside him which isn't working quite right. If I ask about it he gets angry, so I've stopped asking. He likes to give the impression that he's as strong and hale and efficient as he thinks a man ought to be. If he *was* like that, though, I would never have married him. But this is something he must never find out: I don't want him to realize that all his efforts to play the hero are totally wasted.

I met Hubert at a small party. A student called Kranawettreiser had got his doctorate, and since this name suggested goodness knows what to me I went along. Kranawettreiser turned out to be a very ordinary young man who was already drunk by the time we arrived. His fiancée was a friend of mine, and it was she who had invited me. He had studied so incredibly long for his degree that there was good cause for celebration. There were seven or eight people there, mostly students with their girlfriends. Kranawettreiser was the oldest present – he had been allowed to stay on so long at university on account of some illness or other that made him unfit for military service. Everyone envied him this illness. In the background a young man was sitting, changing the records. This was Hubert. He was rather shy and looked bored by all the drunkenness. That immediately gave us something in common. Through the cloud of cigarette smoke his face wore a slightly lost and haughty look. I must have struck him as looking pretty miserable, because he suddenly emerged from the cloud, right in front of me, and asked whether I wouldn't like to go outside for a breath of air. Then he introduced himself, very formal and correct, and in the circumstances it seemed to me rather funny. It was the middle of January but I agreed to his suggestion straight away – snow and cold seemed preferable to the stuffy air inside the room. Nobody noticed us leave but I wouldn't have minded if they had. I cared nothing for my reputation in those days and did exactly what I liked, the only trouble being that when I did it I didn't really like it. I wanted to be different from other people of my age and not to be thought prudish or old fashioned, but deep down inside I had a country girl's abhorrence for the depravity of the big city – it was just that I didn't want it to show. That is probably the reason why I remember so little about this period of my life – it is as if it didn't really belong to me at all.

So out I went with Hubert for a breath of fresh air, imagining that we would probably land up in his digs. I hoped I would eventually manage to talk myself out of the situation because I was tired and not in the right mood. I was depressed because it was winter and because of all the drunks at the party. It soon became apparent, though, that all Hubert had in mind was truly to get some fresh air and have a walk. We wandered through the streets, holding hands, and Hubert told me he only had two week's leave and would then have to go back to join his regiment. He was in uniform, and it annoyed us that every time we passed an officer he had to salute, letting go my hand in the process. We talked to each other properly, not observing the usual rules of the game but chattering openly and without reserve, like two children who have just met up in the playground. It was a wonderful feeling – suddenly, for the first time since I had arrived in this city, I felt I was no longer alone. And it was only then that I realised just how lonely I had been these past few years. The snow fell silently onto the collar of his army greatcoat and onto my little fur collar, and the air smelt almost like it did back home. Hubert accompanied me to Lerchenfelderstrasse where I was living at that time – a street that is nothing like as pretty as the larch trees that gave it its name. It was a long way, but I was used to walking long distances, and we went on holding hands and the snow went on falling, thicker and thicker.

On the doorstep he kissed me – a friendly sort of kiss – and I laid my cheek against his and his face was as cold as mine. I'd always had a weakness for beautiful faces, and Hubert's face looked truly beautiful in the weak lamplight and I would have liked to draw it. But that was not the most important thing; it was the fact that we had talked so much together that counted. By now Hubert knew more about me than anybody else did, because all the people who had really known me were dead. And so it was that I came to believe I now belonged to him. What he felt about the matter I don't know, but anyway we saw each other every day until his leave was up. We married straight after the end of the war, and although we hadn't seen a lot of each other in the interval it was as if we had known each other always. Everything went smoothly, and we were happy and could hardly imagine how we had got on without each other before. And if Hubert had been an orphan like I was, things would never have had to change. Or perhaps they would, I'm not sure, but certainly not so quickly and irreversibly.

This walk through the streets in the cold and the driving snow seems like something out of an old book of legends to me today – a lovely story that is probably quite untrue. To meet each other in the winter, thaw out together gradually, and then to freeze up again at the end – this was our destiny, and for this purpose we were made. If it was just a legend, though, it had a lot of power in it, like all legends do, and later on it helped us build a house for ourselves out of the ruins of our shattered world – a little house, stuccoed all over, its cracks plugged with tow so as not to hear the howling of the wind outside. You *can* hear it, as a matter of fact; of course you can, but not very loud. As lives go, our life together is no worse or more lethal than any other, and it's a good sight more comfortable.

By now Hubert had left again, and my whispered 'Drive carefully' hung in the air unheeded. I watched him from the window as he got into his car. Suddenly he looked back at me and raised his hand: it's his rather melancholy way of waving. His face looked young again and still worth drawing. I'm a bit short-sighted, so I waved back, enraptured, to the young Hubert of the legend. And as I did so I felt a curious feeling, as if an unknown hand had groped inside my brain and forced my head back. It didn't hurt, but it scared me because it was a purely physical sensation and had happened to me before. I think it must have something to do with the circulation and the cause is probably quite natural. Although why the idea of natural causes should reassure us, when the things they cause are either evil or painful or senseless or all three, I fail to understand. What is there to be reassured about? A friendly ghost scares us far worse than a horrible live person, and that is absurd. This yearning for natural explanations must spring from our own profound human stupidity. If only we could rid ourselves of it we could do anything. It's unbelievable what a cramped and impoverished place we have made of the world.

Hubert's smile, or rather the smile of his youthful double, had cheered me up a little, even though it had only fluttered before me hazily though my short-sighted eyes. Maybe, who knows, I could now face the Baroness with more resolve. I went upstairs to change. My stockings were laddered again – that comes of having rough hands from all the housework, but I still prefer rough skin to slippery rubber gloves. I put on a new pair of stockings and an old grey flannel coat and skirt, and over that my oldest overcoat that I usually only wear for funerals. It's the only black coat I possess because I hate everything black. I did all this in order not to look too young or colourful. I put on very little lipstick too for the same reason: the better I look, the more outraged the Baroness becomes, she can't stand people looking nice.

I walked to the tram stop, an eight minutes' walk exactly. Good exercise, or so I tell myself every time I do it. The weather had improved and the slush had melted, the air was very damp with a touch of warmth in it. Grey clouds scudded across the sky: it looked as if it was soon going to rain. I would have to change trams twice, which meant I must be careful to remain alert and not to daydream. The tram was crowded and smelt of wet wool, tobacco, garlic and mothballs, but I felt nothing for my fellow travellers – neither sympathy nor its reverse. I was determined not let my thoughts wander. In the past I'd twice missed a stop and had to walk back to it – I didn't want that to happen today.

This time I managed all right and got out where I was meant to: Lerchenfeldstrasse, the ugly street with the pretty name. I passed a flower shop with roses, violets and carnations in its window, and thought briefly of buying some but then changed my mind. I like flowers, and couldn't bear the thought of them being stuffed into a vase with no water in it and left there to wilt, the way the Baroness was sure to treat them. They'd find a better home with some other passer-by. Years ago I had made the mistake of buying her a budgerigar – it had died of mysterious symptoms one week later. You should never give pets or flowers to the murderously inclined. So I bought her a box of chocolates instead and walked on with a clear conscience: chocolates are for biting into; just the thing for the Baroness.

She lives in a big building dating from the turn of the 19th century. The house has a lift but I don't like using lifts, so I always walk up to the third floor where her apartment is situated. The climb made me slightly out of breath and I waited a couple of minutes before ringing the bell. I didn't want the Baroness to catch me at a disadvantage – in fact I didn't want her to catch me at all and would much rather have turned and fled – but as I stood there a noise like a hurricane came from behind the door, a kind of pounding, roaring, stamping noise: she was evidently already expecting me. She flung open the door, dragged me inside and, gripping me by the shoulders, clasped me to her bosom. There is something dubious and weird about this bosom, it isn't soft like it should be but as hard as stone, and it creaks slightly as if it was filled with sawdust. But it's real all right: the Baroness favours low necklines and of necessity I've seen enough of that bosom to know that it is real. All the same there is something not quite human about its texture. I have puzzled over this often and in vain.

After being trapped for a while in her iron embrace and kissed repeatedly on the mouth, I was at last able to shift my head far enough backwards so that the next kiss merely grazed my cheek. She is the only person who kisses me on the mouth, and once, in doing so, she chipped a little splinter off my top left incisor. I thought that was going a bit too far. Since then I clamp my mouth shut and try to breathe through my nose – no easy feat because it is usually squashed by various parts of the Baroness's anatomy.

For years I have asked myself what this greeting means. I can only explain it this way: that it provides a momentary outlet for all the Baroness's cravings rolled into one. It is not me, that is, whom she sees in that instant as holding back from her, she sees the whole world, and it's not just holding back, it is closing itself against her, implacably and for ever. I could smell lavender, face powder, and the faintly metallic smell of the Baroness's body. She yanked me out of my coat and drove me into the sitting room with sweeping movements of her hands, like someone shooing chickens into a run. In this old fashioned living room of hers nothing has changed from as long back as I can remember. It is a hideous room exactly suited to its owner. There is not one single chair on which you can sit without enduring agonies. My feet go to sleep, then my back begins to ache, then it's the turn of my shoulders, and finally I begin to feel as if my bones were boring through my backside onto the seat below. At that point I know I must go because the pain soon becomes unbearable. The

Baroness is better upholstered than I am, naturally, but even so I don't know how she can stand it.

Anyway, now we were sitting down and the torture could begin. The Baroness had placed her hands on the table with outspread fingers. Her hands are neither wrinkled nor freckled – they are fat and shiny and the fingertips are stubby and splayed. She must be sixty-four or sixty-five but she looks much younger. No, not younger exactly, more as if she had been embalmed round about the age of fifty by a true artist in the trade. Since I've known her, which must be about twenty-seven years now, she has hardly changed at all: she is not perishable or breakable in any way, she's simply scary. In actual fact she's not a real Baroness at all, she's just a very rich daughter of an upper middle class family who happens to have married a Baron. In each room hangs an oil painting of her, depicting her in the various stages of her life: first as a young girl, then as a young wife, and finally as widow. Reputedly she was once a great beauty, but in her pictures she always wears the same look: that of a man eater. You get the feeling that if you could fend her off with a pair of fire-tongs she would perhaps be easier to handle.

'How are you, Aunt Lily?' I asked. I always say that, it acts as a cue. For a long while afterwards I don't have to say anything else, just stare into her large, pink-powdered face and look attentive. One minute later we had already reached the subject where all conversations with her automatically wind up, namely that of the late Baron. I did my best to hear nothing while at the same time appearing to follow every word. The Baron has been dead these past forty years but she won't allow him to stay dead, because it's her hatred of him that keeps her strong and vital and blooming. And since I've been hearing such terrible things about him for so long I have formed a very clear picture of him in my head: that of ill, luckless man who sold himself for a lot of money. I see him sitting alone in a room, his skin a waxen yellow, his hands trembling, and his dark eyes fixed on the drawer of his desk wherein lies his only hope of escape: his army revolver. Day and night he is besieged by the shrieks of this woman to whom, once, on his wedding night, in a drunken trance, he was imprudent enough to unite himself. According to the Baroness he later turned out to be a great womanizer, but I don't believe it possible: his career as a lover must surely have ended that night.

And then, finally, one day, his hand reaches out to the drawer, and . . . I have a slight weakness for the Baron. I particularly like the fact that he never gave his wife a child. That's a nice trait in his character, even if it smacks slightly of cheating. To save up a lot of money and then have no children to leave it to may be a sensible course but it's not a very generous one. All in all, a rather sad life. For the fun he had in his youth he paid heavily. He must have been a rather careless person, not very bright, perhaps something of a coward. Time and hatred have built him into a demon of huge proportions but this he can never have been. The whole story is like something out of a cheap magazine – unreal, unnatural, like the sawdust bosom of the Baroness herself.

I sometimes wonder how I ever could have stomached her, but in those days the little room she rented out to me – it was originally a maid's room – seemed like a blessing from heaven. I even had the use of the bathroom and the kitchen, and after I'd been there a week I was allowed to call her Aunt Lily. Then she started on her dreadful reminiscences, thrashing around all over the place and screaming, and I began to fear her. Although to give her her due, once, during a freezing cold winter in the war, she took care of me when I had the flu, gave me aspirin and wrapped me up in a damp linen cloth. True, she did it with a brutal roughness, but that's the way she does everything. And the cure must have worked because I was soon on my feet again, although the thought of another damp cloth around me may have speeded my recovery.

In those days too – and this is an important point – she used to keep silent for hours on end and let me sleep, which is why I mistook her for so long for a human being. Then, a little later on, there came the time when she would cling to me in the air-raid shelter with her teeth chattering, and down there, amid the smells of sweat and terror and potatoes, she didn't scream either, she whimpered. Her whimpering made more impression on me than the raids – not because there was anything wrong in it, but because she clung so hard she almost broke my ribs. It was a bad time altogether.

Once she even wrote to me in Pruschen; she must have wangled the address out of Hubert somehow. She wrote: 'Be brave, my poor child. Men are to blame for everything, I hope you realise that now.' And then came a long litany of the Baron's abominations. I never answered her, and she never wrote again either: a person who doesn't answer stops existing so far as the Baroness is concerned. Then, later, when I came back, we met up one day by chance in the street and she grabbed hold of me and whisked me back into her life. It was a lucky day for her. From then on I took to visiting her every fourth Tuesday of the month: I really can't be quite right in the head.

The Baroness never mentions Hubert to me, which is very clever of her. She can say nothing nice about him, you see, since in her eyes he is a smaller edition of the Baron, but on the other hand she can say nothing nasty for fear of offending me and perhaps losing me altogether. This she on no account wishes to do: not because I mean anything to her personally but because I am the thing that sits at her table and onto which she can unload all her rubbish. Everything in the world exists for her only in relation to herself, and for that reason her world is minute.

She thumped her fist down onto the table and the tea things clattered loudly. Had I been listening to her properly? Of course I hadn't. 'He was a swine,' she shouted, 'Nothing but a swine,' and stared at me hard.

It is very strange that her eyes – little round yellow eyes – never show any signs of the anger that racks her body. I've never seen such expressionless eyes. 'Don't get so worked up, Aunt Lily,' I urged her. 'He's been dead for so long, and he's really not worth it.' That was a craven utterance on my part, but it's hard not to be craven in her proximity, I am no hero.

'I'll make him pay for it,' she yelled, still staring at me with those yellow eyes that didn't see anything at all. Then she started crying. Not from sadness but from hate. But where does the hate end and the sadness begin? 'He was so handsome,' she added, 'such a fine looking man.' She was almost whispering at this point and it made my flesh creep; I prefer it when she yells. I was quite frightened: she must know what I really think of her deep down. One day it might strike her fancy to bash me over the head with the wrought iron lamp stand, only she can't afford to because then I would be dead and she would have to yell at herself.

Now she was lost in reminiscences of her own countless erotic triumphs – a reaction against the Baron's indifference, she is careful to specify: I am on no account to think that she remained faithful to him. I can't believe a word of it: no way are men so courageous. When I ask her what has become of all these men, her imagination fails her. Some of them may indeed be dead and others may have gone abroad, the way she says, but not a whole regiment, surely? When I lived with her I never saw a man come near the place, except for the odd workman. I used to hope that she would indeed eventually find a man for herself – a German officer, say, who didn't know her reputation – but I hoped in vain.

I sat quite still and wondered to myself why it was that I didn't just get up and leave, or else laugh out loud and expose the whole story as nonsense. Cautiously I stole a glance at the clock on the wall: one hour still to go. Gradually the Baroness's voice transformed itself into the murmuring of the sea with an occasional breaking of a wave against the shore. I tried to imagine myself back in the loft, and in my mind's eye set about drawing a bird. My fingers moved slightly as if they were holding a pencil, and I felt myself secure and shielded. I was almost happy, but then there came the crashing of a wave. 'What do you say to that? He never even left a farewell note.'

My mouth answered for me: 'Perhaps he was just too unhappy, Aunt Lily. Unhappy people never write letters.'

'Nonsense!' She shrieked, 'He wasn't unhappy; he did it out of spite, out of pure spite. Don't try to defend him, he was a swine, that's all.'

Cold menace lay in her voice, so I silently begged the Baron's forgiveness and said, 'You're right, he was a swine.' My feet had gone to sleep long ago, my back hurt, and now I could feel my seat bones starting to dig into my flesh. I was so depressed I could think of nothing more to say. Then, to my horror, I heard myself give a soft laugh: I was evidently close to breaking point.

'What is there to laugh about?' said the Baroness icily.

'I'm laughing,' I tried to explain, 'because human beings are so stupid.'

For some extraordinary reason this pleased her. She launched straight away into three of her favourite anecdotes: one about a foolish cook of hers who had had an illegitimate child, one about foolish nephew who had married beneath him, and the third about a foolish housekeeper who hadn't wanted to let her old dog be put down. I noticed that my forehead was damp with the effort of listening, although it was cold in the room. The Baroness goes sparingly on the coal, she considers fifteen degrees centigrade quite warm enough. She stews comfortably in her hatred and douses it with a lot of iced water; she downs litres of the stuff, but the fire is never extinguished. When she dies, where will all the hatred go, I wonder? Will it die with her? I doubt it; most likely it will stay in the room and then slowly filter through the chinks in the windowpanes to join the big cloud of hatred that hangs over the city permanently.

'Between his eyebrows,' the Baroness was now saying, 'he had a mole, it looked like a caste mark. Beware those who bear the mark.' Her fist, which was still on the table, firmly clenched, loosened up and became a plump, helpless hand. 'He never liked me,' she sighed. 'I was young and rich and beautiful but he preferred sleeping with his whores. Can you understand that?'

I could understand only too well but I shook my head and looked puzzled.

'Of course you can't,' she said, 'No normal person can. He was mad and he was a swine – a mad swine.' The description seemed to please her, she repeated it twice. As she did so she laughed and a vein in her cheek swelled menacingly. She will die soon, I thought to myself, and I will be free of her. Really I suppose I should have said something comforting, but I simply couldn't. I felt wretched: the place smelt of evil old things, mummies or suchlike, that were shut away in some chest. The Baroness didn't notice the state I was in: she never notices what's going on inside me because for her I am only a thing, not a person. You have to shoot yourself in order to show her you're fed up with her. Now she had started on the catalogue of the various ways in which she had contemplated eliminating the Baron: poison, assault, strangling, electrocution in the bath, and so forth.

'Forgive me, Aunt Lily,' I said, 'I really must be going now. I'll be back in four weeks' time.'

She crumpled like a burst balloon. I kissed her fleetingly on the forehead and a smell of hot metal stung my nose, lightly overlaid with a whiff of lavender and talcum powder. She always smells that way – of metal and burning – and it fits her character perfectly. She didn't accompany me to the door, she never does, which meant I could make a quick escape. I could imagine the carpets and furniture being afraid now that they were alone in the room with her. I wouldn't like to be the person who buys them in a junk shop when she is dead. Nobody should buy old furnishings, there's too much history attached to them.

As I sat in the tram it struck me for the first time that although the Baroness always lays the table for tea there is never any tea served. Only that iced water that she keeps gulping down, and she doesn't offer me any of that either. I wonder if she ever removes the tea things or if she leaves them there, untouched, ready for my next visit? I'd really like to know why it is that I shall be back there in four weeks' time, sitting at her table, yes, I'd really like to know.

The moment I got home I went straight to the bathroom and drew myself a bath. I lay there in the tub, motionless in the warm water, for a good quarter of an hour and watched the little bubbles gather on my skin and then slowly rise to the surface. Five minutes used to be enough to wash away all traces of the Baroness, now I need a full fifteen. Suddenly I had a flash of insight: I am a monster, I realised, a monster that wants to stalk through the woods, free and alone, and cannot even bear so much as the touch of a branch on its skin. There'd be nothing wrong with that, if it weren't for the fact that every so often the monster wants to be loved and cosseted and has to grovel, whining, back to the world of men.

The thought disappeared as quickly as it had come, leaving no trace save for a stinging feeling in my cheek. I put on an old housecoat and went to lay the table, then Hubert called and said he wouldn't be back till later. I replaced the receiver feeling pleased and disappointed at the same time: pleased because it meant I could now go up to the loft, and disappointed because the loft has recently become a threatening place for me. Slowly I made my way upstairs.

December 2nd

It is snowing. I feel empty and peaceful. For the first time since I've been here I can understand what I read. I get books sent to me from the lending library. I order only historical works; I can't read poetry or novels. For the past week I've been reading about the rise and fall of the Roman Empire, but up till now I've had to start afresh from the beginning every day because I couldn't understand a word, the meaning just wouldn't get through to me. Yesterday was the first day I could read properly, so the rise and fall of the Roman Empire is like the pattern of my own life.

The wood outside stands heavy and rigid under its wet coat of snow. Every so often a lump of snow falls to the ground and you can see a little patch of green from the fir saplings underneath. The

Roman Empire touches me deeply. I pity it as I would pity a huge, magnificent wild beast, asleep in the Steppes. As it sleeps its flanks heave and sink, and it has no notion that one day it will be annihilated. It is good for me to let myself feel pity – for the Roman Empire at least – because it is a safe kind of pity and doesn't really hurt. I feel a little better; soon I may even be able to make it to the village. The moment I think about this, though, I start worrying again, so I try not to think about it. That is the reason I am here: to think things over in peace and quiet, but I'm afraid I may not be cut out for thinking. I didn't know that about myself before, but here the defect becomes evident.

Hubert wants to come here on Boxing Day. Christmas obviously he has to spend with little Ferdinand. I am not looking forward to his visit. He is my husband but I can't somehow feel any more that he is my husband. I have no longing for his touch. Deep inside me there is a core of coldness. I think more about the Roman Empire than I do about Hubert. The Empire is long since dead, and you can let yourself love dead things without the risk of being punished for it. Hubert is far too alive. I imagine him placing his hand on my cheek, and the feeling is weird. Why should he ever to do a thing like that, and why should my cheek ever be pleased about it? It's so long since anyone touched me that, if they did, I think I might splinter into a thousand little ice crystals. It would be unbearable. Everything that has passed between Hubert and me seems impossible to me today.

To begin with, when the deafness started, I used to cling to him hard: I couldn't hear him, maybe, but his was still the warm comforting body that I knew. I could see his face and smell his smell. He must have found it disconcerting: I could read the shock and bewilderment in his eyes. Maybe he was even frightened of me. I can understand him now very well. I can understand his mother too, who wanted nothing more to do with me – her only son, married to a deaf woman. I grew more and more afraid; when visitors came I would run away and lock myself in my room. I didn't belong with them any more; I had been torn from the world of normal people. I didn't know *what* I was.

Once, just for a moment, Hubert even thought it would have been better if I hadn't survived that night of the howling sirens. How do I know this? I know it because I've always had the knack of reading other people's thoughts. It's a very inconvenient thing to have: there is a sudden switch and I am right inside the other person's head, and then out again, horrified by what I have seen. It happens very seldom, but that time it happened all right. Hubert was sitting at his desk, studying. I entered the room, trying to be as quiet as possible – I was always careful about how I moved because I was terrified of making a lot of noise by mistake. The room was filled with sunshine, and I stood still, in a broad beam of motes, not wanting to startle him. I could feel my hair shimmering in the light. It seemed to me impossible to go one single step further. It wasn't only that I couldn't hear, I hardly dared speak, either, because I didn't know what my voice sounded like. I felt myself a stranger in the world – an alien thing that had no business to be there. And yet only two months earlier it had been my world, and I had felt safe and comfortable in it. So safe and comfortable that I sometimes I had trouble believing it.

Suddenly Hubert noticed there was someone standing behind him and turned round. He saw me standing in the light, in this shaft of little shining dust particles, and his eyes filled with pain. I was inside his head and I knew he wished I was dead. I don't remember what happened next. From that moment on I no longer wanted to stay. Hubert was against me leaving, but I could tell that secretly he was relieved by my decision.

And then Madam Magistrate got busy. It was the first time she had showed me any friendliness whatsoever, she even offered to pay for a sanatorium and patted me on the back to comfort me. I sat there motionless and said I didn't want to go a sanatorium, I just wanted to go somewhere where I didn't have to mix with other people. I could see she liked that idea: it would be cheaper, and she was tight with her money. It was quite true, too, I did want to be alone, and I couldn't bear the thought of Hubert feeling indebted to his mother for her footing the sanatorium bill. So it has worked out better this way all round.

That's why I don't want Hubert to come here: I don't want to see him upset, and I don't want to know that he wishes me dead, and I don't want to be reminded of little Ferdinand – hopefully he'll soon forget me. I want to go on sitting here in this old leather chair, reading about the Roman Empire, and every so often I want to look out of the window at the snow, lying on the firs, and I want no one to touch me because I don't want to shatter to pieces. The doctor says I have done this to myself, and only I can undo it again. I can't understand this. Why should I have done such a thing to myself? But if he's right, then I'll just have to wait until this weird creature inside me decides it's time to start hearing again. I can't force anything to happen, because the creature will not be forced. I will have to be patient.

December 10th

The publishers I occasionally do freelance work for have written asking me if I'd like to illustrate a book about insects. It'll be a book for the general reader, they say, so I shan't have to bother about depicting every little feeler. But I'm very precise about feelers, so I must set about getting some good material to copy. I'm going to accept: insects are exactly right for me just now; they too are different from all other living creatures. Besides, I don't want Hubert to pay for my keep indefinitely. It's true that I live here very cheaply, but Hubert has to start making a new life for himself and for that he will need a lot of money.

I have brought my painting materials with me; it was Hubert's idea actually, he said it would help take my mind off things. Only he didn't say it, of course, he wrote it on a sheet of paper. He bought a thick note pad for this purpose and every evening we would burn all the sheets he'd used during the day; every day there was less and less to burn.

No, I'd rather remain in the Roman Empire. I dream a lot nowadays about ruined cities, and about landscapes with no people in them, just weather-beaten statues. I wander from one statue to the other and they stare at me out of their white eye sockets – they can see me and they don't mind me being there among them. In the dream all is still, and I feel sleepy and make my way down into some deep vaults that are warm and dry and whose walls are covered with ancient inscriptions that I cannot read. In my dream the fact that I can't read them is somehow reassuring: I know they are not there for me to read. I lie down on the floor, which is covered in grass, and fall asleep. It's not really a sleep but a state of unconsciousness that is permanent. Just before I drop off I always feel very happy.

In the daytime this dream seems threatening and disturbing, but at night it is all very familiar and I feel quite at home in it, and safe, as if I had completed a long and tiring journey. More at home than I did in my grandfather's house. I've tried drawing the landscape and the statues but I can't manage it, and this reassures me in the same way as my incapacity to read the inscriptions.

The gamekeeper brings in wood and piles it in front of the stove. From the look in his eyes and the sour smelling snorts he gives I can tell he thinks me a useless female, and he's not entirely wrong.

I've made up my mind to go to the village myself soon so that he won't have to keep doing my shopping. But why haven't I done so yet? It would be so easy. You go into the shop and slide your list over the counter to the assistant, at the same time giving a wide smile. My smile has always worked on people, always aroused their sympathy, why should it stop working now for the mere fact that I can't hear them?

For the present, though, I'd rather not go to the village – soon, maybe, but not today and not tomorrow either.

The gamekeeper has a cat that lives in the stable. Sometimes I see it slip across the road, all sinuous and grey. I shouldn't think he gives it more than the odd saucer of milk; it's not allowed to enter the house and it doesn't even try. It would be nice to have a cat, cats are warm and soft and full of life. I could become fond of it. But then, when I leave, it would be on its own again with the gamekeeper. Better not to learn the meaning of fondness, because then you don't miss it when it's gone.

But who says I will ever leave this place anyway?

January 10th

Today I went in the wood. Beauty and a frozen stillness. Nothing to distract me, neither the whispering of the trees nor the squeak of my shoes on the snow. I have a very vivid memory of that dry, squeaky sound. The silence lends an air of unreality to everything; I feel as if I were a spirit living in the snowy wood. Not an animal to be seen. Where can they all have gone to? Maybe they are under the snow-capped bushes, or else in burrows at their roots, or in the hollows of the trees. A lot of tits and finches come and feed at my window but I have seen no birds at all in the wood. It could be that my tread scares them away; I mustn't forget that I make as much noise as everyone else. Or it could be that they are huddled in the forks of branches, there in the snowy white penumbra – little living creatures gathered into a warm ball so as not to disperse the waning heat, while above the clouds the implacable bird god with his red feathers goes slowly on his rounds. One blink of his black eyes, and thousands of tiny claws seize up and loosen their holds on the branches; and later their remains will lie on the snow, their grey feathers frosted over, claws spread wide, and in the wood it will be a little colder than before, and it will be as if nothing had happened, nothing at all.

My hands and feet are cold and stiff. When I think of the dead birds I feel very little heat inside myself. I am certain now that the gamekeeper is afraid of me. When he brings in the wood and sees me curled in my armchair he turns his head the other way so as not to have to look at me. It's almost comical. But then he's an ignorant and superstitious person, so why shouldn't he be afraid of me? Even Hubert is afraid of me.

I was right, Hubert should never have come. In the past the essential thing for us was to be able to talk to one another. So now it scares him not to know what I'm thinking or feeling, since those things can't very well be written down on a scrap of notepaper. Hubert, the only child, who had at last found a playmate, feels betrayed. The playmate has turned into a deaf and silent doll who has abandoned him. He looked tired and wore a curious smile on his face all the time: strained and suffering. He hardly ever summoned up courage to switch the smile off; it acted like a kind of screen between us – a magic curtain that prevented us from seeing the alien element in the other's familiar face. All night we clung together, holding hands. I could sense his anguish seeping into my fingers. It was a moonless night and I hope, at least while sleeping, that he put away the smile. I didn't dare remove my hand, and I was glad when, after a last despairing hug, he finally fell asleep.

I lay awake until morning, all the while thinking how the bed was really too small for the two of us. We definitely hadn't grown any taller or fatter, and the bed was wider than any we had slept in in the past, but then it had not used to bother us and now it did.

When dawn broke Hubert was still asleep, and I could observe his face. It didn't look young any more, the streak of haughtiness had gone and tiredness had taken its place. From nose to mouth two lines had etched themselves, not deeply but visible all the same. I felt very guilty, I didn't know why. A little later on Hubert wrote a note: 'I'll be back to see you soon. Try to hold out a little longer.' He's got his eye on an apartment, and on some rooms that'll do for an office. And one day we'll all three of us be together again. He wrote that too, and he begged me to be patient. Which was odd; I hadn't uttered an impatient word. Then he left for the station. After he'd gone I burned everything he had written. The way the gamekeeper so painstakingly does with his notes – he doesn't want anything of his to fall into my hands; or so I imagine, it is not easy to guess what goes on in that primitive mind.

February 14th

The snow is still here but it's not quite so cold. I have finished the insects – grasshoppers, bumblebees, rose chafers, iridescent flies and fierce looking hornets, dragonflies too, plus many others. These creatures are not meant to be understood and therefore they are easy to draw.

As a child I was frightened of mole crickets, probably because the country people hate them so much. They used to say they did so much damage that if you saw one when you were riding you must get off your horse to crush it. With much reluctance and disgust I crushed many of them myself: to me they were the embodiment of everything ugly and wicked. Now for the first time I had to draw one – it looked nightmarish and at last I realised it was my own ugliness and wickedness I was drawing: five centimetres of evil on yellow paper. I tore it up and drew another one; it filled me with pity. A mole cricket is not wicked, nor is it nightmarish. Its brown colouring isn't ugly, it is the colour of the earth. It is a poor little plump insect that is hated and persecuted because it happens to feed off roots and unwittingly gets in mankind's way. It looked lost and bewildered – a creature that cannot understand why it is hated and persecuted. I took it to my heart, and it turned into the subject of my best insect picture. Never again shall a rider get off his horse to crush a mole cricket. I like it far better than the shimmering rose chafer or the golden hornets that the rest of the world admires.

With my insects it doesn't matter that they look so lonely. Each of them is enveloped in an aura of apartness – the same aura that envelopes me. They look comfortable that way, but the same does not apply to my birds. I'm sure it's possible to draw a bird that isn't all on its own: that I can't do so depends entirely on me. I don't shrink from using tricks sometimes, but even so I can't manage it. For example, once I drew a pair of titmice perched on a branch with their little heads turned towards each other – the drawing may have deceived other people but it didn't deceive me. I couldn't tell what they were looking at but they certainly weren't aware of one another's presence. No, it has got to be a single bird, and everything about it must proclaim: 'I am not the only bird in the world; when I sing millions of other birds perk up and answer me; my song is their song and my warmth glows in their bodies, we are one and the same being; I'm a happy bird because I'm not alone.'

When I'd finished reading all these pages I took them down to the cellar and shoved them in the burner. Quite why I burned them I'm not sure, it could just have been a way of keeping things tidy. I want my drawings in the loft, and nothing but my drawings: this dangerous material has no right to be there. Because it *is* dangerous. It brings back things I thought I'd long since forgotten. In my memory the time I spent in Pruschen has become like a blurred nightmare, and I don't want to be reminded of the details any more. On the other hand, I can't quite bring myself to destroy the pages without reading them, because I need to know what else I am destroying with them. Yesterday I still had the feeling I was reading the sad story of a totally unknown young woman, but today she'd drawn closer to me and was trying to draw me back into her life. I want nothing to do with her, though; I don't even like her.

I know beyond a doubt that tomorrow I will receive yet another yellow envelope: it can't stop that easily. Or can it? Either way, whatever comes, I shall read it all before burning it: I never go back on my decisions, even when they're stupid. It's a kind of compulsion with me – a dangerous trait in my character that has done me a good deal of harm in the past. Once I've made up my mind I can't unmake it. It could be that without knowing it I'm slightly mad, and I shouldn't wonder if I were: I belong to a generation that has been driven mad in its entirety by the aftermath of events it was not equipped to deal with. That no generation, for that matter, is equipped to deal with. Because there do exist events of that magnitude. To our children we must seem odd and hard to understand. Nor will they ever understand us, either, not unless they too come to find themselves, one day, swept up by similar events and left stranded in their past, the way we were. Outsiders cannot understand such things, only insiders can.

That is why it is so important for Hubert and me to be patient with each other, and to weigh our words carefully, and to live as if nothing had ever happened. That is why it doesn't surprise me that Hubert should sometimes sit at his desk for hours on end – doing nothing, just sitting staring into space. What do I know about his defence mechanisms? What do I know about those memories of his that he has sealed off so tightly, but that nevertheless keep threatening to break out? There are periods of his life that he's never talked to me about at all – those periods when I was in the air raid shelter and he was in the trenches. All his life he has laboured to forget these things, and if he's become a bit odd in the process, well, who better than I can understand that? For a couple of years we were misled – by our youth and the mere fact of having survived – into thinking all would be well; but we couldn't stay young forever, and I was the first to break down. Hubert would never have written about his sufferings the way I did, and for that I admire him.

As regards the man whom I think is responsible for sending the yellow envelopes, he is behaving much as I would have expected: even then, seventeen years ago, he was unbalanced, in fact, worse, he was raving mad. It's not for me to criticize his madness – he has a right to it the way we all do. I'm not frightened of him, either, though I easily could be. It would be foolish to worry – let him do what he wants, whatever may bring him relief.

I went up to the sitting room and sat down in an armchair. I felt really annoyed now, but only because this business had prevented me from drawing all week, and drawing is vital to me. I laid my hands under my head and fell into a deep and dreamless sleep which lasted until Hubert came back and woke me up. I gazed round the room sleepily and realised that I was not really at home here. But at the same time I felt I'd rather be not at home here than not at home anywhere else, and must therefore consider myself very lucky.

Wednesday

Wednesday is my day for cleaning the house. I do one room thoroughly – a different one each time – and the others I just tidy up. I suppose I could easily find someone to help me out but I'm not very good when it comes to helpers: I get too involved with them and can't keep the distance I'd like. And anyway, doing the chores makes me feel useful. Hubert works hard to keep the house going, so why shouldn't I? Manual work can only be good for me at my age, seeing that I don't take any other form of excercise. On Wednesdays Hubert always lunches in town. Sometimes he meets up with a certain Dr Melichar, an acquaintance of his whom he never invites here. He's probably afraid I would find him droll or boring. Even if I didn't say so, he would know the way I felt, he's very sensitive on that score. But I have a soft spot for this Dr Melichar as he seems to cheer Hubert up. Hubert is more of a man's man really; he's a bit chary of women, he doesn't like their chatter, or what he refers to as their chatter. It's understandable when you think how long he suffered under his mother's sway. Wednesday, then, is for him Dr Melichar day, and for me clean-out day – an arrangement that suits us both.

Being me, I stick to a very tight plan. If I didn't I'd never get finished, or else I'd gradually stop cleaning altogether because basically it's a task I loathe. I merely pretend to myself that I enjoy it, since pretending is a part of my system. In the morning I do the main rooms, and in the afternoon the kitchen, bathroom, store rooms and veranda.

The loft I clean on a different day so as to make a sharp division between it and the rest of the house. No member of the family has ever slept there, only the cook, Serafine.

Once a fortnight I set aside a day for window cleaning. Light laundry I do on a day to day basis, the rest of our stuff I send out. I'm a rotten ironer, men's shirts in particular defeat me, and I'm much better at heavy jobs than fiddly ones. I dislike sewing too, and any kind of handiwork that involves sitting. Even when I'm painting or drawing I have to keep getting up and taking a walk. I close my eyes while I do this so as to see things clearer, and I often bump into pieces of furniture and bruise myself. I can only see things properly with my eyes shut.

Hubert can sit still for hours. I used to feel sorry for him when I saw him doing this, but it was quite unnecessary since he seems to enjoy it. It's a mystery to me, but he's evidently comfortable that way. He can concentrate on a subject so hard that he doesn't notice what's going on around him. For me concentration is far more difficult, I can only do it when I'm alone, and even then only for a very short time. I think when I'm on the move, and my thoughts move around with me, darting and wandering all over the place. But I can't *not* think, either. Hubert can, I can tell that from his face: it goes totally empty and takes on a slightly foolish look, making him look more handsome than usual. And since I like his face when it's asleep or empty-looking, I can imagine to myself then that I love him. At any rate he's the only man I could ever bear to have around me for any length of time. It helps, of course, that he's out of the house for most of the day. Ferdinand, in contrast, is a disruptive unsettling presence, although a welcome one; and Ilse can get on my nerves sometimes because she's so loud and healthy. But then they are my children, if they annoy me sometimes, they do so in the way a leg of mine would, or an arm. They are not my partners, though; I must make no mistake about this: my only partner is Hubert. Many women would find him an impossible partner, but for me he is the right one. He's around, and yet he's not around, and he never comes too close.

Once upon a time it was different. We were closer to one another then, sometimes too close. But neither of us would have been able to hold out that way for long, we were not accustomed to closeness or unity with another being. I sometimes wonder whether that could have been one of the reasons for my illness. But that is a loft-thought that I must chase away at once. I know little about Hubert, and that little is already too much. Sometimes I feel it's slightly indecent to know so much about one's partner.

I switched the hoover on and let it purr. Immediately my thoughts began to swarm around everywhere.

The house looks different now from what it used to. Hubert has sold almost all our old furniture; some of the prettier bits went to Ferdinand to help him furnish his apartment, and the remaining ones weren't old enough to be pretty. The only piece Hubert kept was his father's writing desk – a dark, heavy affair that I can't manage to move on my own. I never complain about this, though, because Hubert loves this desk and is always careful that it doesn't get scratched, or that someone doesn't put a wet glass on it by mistake. He never lets cigarette ash fall on the surface either, as could so easily happen. In fact he treats it like a stand-in for his father, whom he wouldn't have liked to have seen scratched or burned either.

Hubert seldom speaks about his father, but when you see the way he cares for that desk, their relationship is clear.

It saddens me sometimes that he never kept one single thing belonging to his mother. It's true, her furniture was hideous, but still, he might have kept an ornament or something. It's not that I pity her in the slightest; I just wish for Hubert's sake that they had got on better with one another. In the end I suppose I was one of the main causes of their estrangement.

The elder Ferdinand was very sweet to me from the start. At the time I met him he was still an attractive man, very dark and thin, and elegant in his ways. His expression was rather sombre, but he could be very charming, and there was something slightly enigmatic about him. I could have become very fond of him, I think, but I only saw him three times in all. He died suddenly when he was sixty-four, while sitting at his desk. His wife was at the hairdresser's when it happened; Serafine the cook was out at the market; and when his body was found it was already cold. He had whisked himself off at just the right moment, in time to avoid all the discomforts of old age, and in particular that of having to endure being taken care of in his dotage by his wife.

The hoover purred, and I felt love for the dear old Ferdinand who had kissed my hand when I was a young girl still, and I let the love waft through the room and settle on his desk in a cloud. Poor Hubert, he will never be the man his father was. He doesn't like women, he merely needs them, and he doesn't really like life either, for him it is a piece of homework that some unknown teacher has set him, and that he can't get his head round, no matter how hard he tries. And try he does. Ferdinand is like the elder Ferdinand; Hubert has merely inherited surface traits. Hubert is smaller than his father, for one thing, and of much lighter build. He doesn't give an impression of sombreness and elegance, he just comes over as being correct and dry.

I went into the kitchen and emptied the bag of the vacuum cleaner. Recently things have taken a strange turn: Hubert in fact is growing more like his father, and that's not a good thing, he ought to grow more like himself. It worries me slightly, although I realise there's nothing to be done about it – things never go the way they should. But I sometimes wonder what has happened to the real Hubert. Like a good actor he plays the part of a thin, elegant man of sombre mien, but where is his real self lurking?

The hoover suddenly stalled with a roaring noise and freed me from the disturbing thought that maybe there had never been a real Hubert – only embryo shoots of personality that had withered before reaching maturity. I fiddled with the hoover, gave it a random shake that sometimes works, and the howl once more turned to a friendly purr. Yes, that was the truth of the matter, and Hubert's hard outer shell had provided him with the only form he could take.

I ran the hoover under the beds, irritated as usual by the fact that it doesn't reach far enough. A vague sense of malaise pervaded me. There are always feathers under the beds, the duvet linings must be getting thin. We ought to have new ones, but they're probably very expensive. I decided to forget about the feathers and had no trouble doing so.

When I was young I was convinced that Madame Magistrate hadn't got a soul. Quite what I meant by soul, I'm no longer sure, but I must have had a fair idea in order to have denied her one with such assurance. Probably it was because all that that woman seemed to consist of was a cold, hard, impenetrable surface. I never had the feeling I was speaking to a real person, insofar as we spoke to one another at all. I knew she didn't like me, but even her dislike had nothing personal about it since she hardly liked anybody. I was merely an impediment to her son's future, or to the future, at any rate, that she had mapped out for him; I was a factor to be eliminated. I wonder what she would have done about me if, after a mere four years of marriage, I hadn't so obligingly gone and eliminated myself?

Certain traits in her character I noticed all right, but then so did anyone who came in contact with her. She was domineering, miserly and suspicious. She was a bad wife to her husband and a bad mother to Hubert, but she was a very good grandmother to Ferdinand, never bossing him around and occasionally showering him with presents. In her last years she must have told him a great deal about her childhood and youth, because he knows things about her that Hubert has never heard. Hubert knows nothing, for example, about her family and relatives, while Ferdinand knows masses. She was one of eight children, her father was a civil servant and earned very little money. To enable the sons to study, the girls were obliged to stay at home and live in poverty. I don't think she ever really got over it.

After her marriage, which introduced her into higher social circles, she paid no more attention to her family and never mentioned them. Not until her old age did she dig these things up again to tell them to her grandson. Apparently as a child she had a rough time defending herself against her many equally combative brothers and sisters. The thing that seemed to have embittered her most was having to wear her elder sisters' cast off clothes, and this right up to the day of her wedding. That was presumably why in later life she set such store by clothes and jewels.

She was a good looking woman, tall and slim, with very thick, dark hair which, more than hair, resembled a black enamel helmet. She looked somehow sharply defined and highly polished. That all this didn't add up to real elegance depended, I suspect, on her passion for jewellery – she always wore a couple of pieces too many. Flowers and animals she couldn't abide; in her house I never saw so much as a plant, and Ferdinand senior clearly suffered from her ban on his keeping a dog. She collected a lot of copper and porcelain knickknacks, and all these treasures she sold before she died, along with her jewels. I assume this was because she couldn't bear the thought of their coming to me. If so, it wasn't a clever move, since she lost money over the transaction, but I'm glad she made it.

I didn't know much about people when I first met her, all I could sense was the aura they gave off, and hers was of polished marble. I can't say I hated her or disliked her; for me she was like a disturbing but fascinating painting, and I used to stare at her for minutes on end when I was sure I could do so without being noticed. All I reproached her for was having made Hubert so unhappy – because he was unhappy when I met him. He'd used up so much strength in his youth, trying to break free from her – and all in vain, since she was by far the stronger of the two.

After he'd found me, all went well for a while. We sub-rented an apartment, which used up all the money Hubert's father had left him. Later on I realised how easy it would have been for the old woman to have helped us out, but at the time neither of us had any idea of how much money she possessed. I suppose in the end it worked out better that way: it is important to Hubert to know that everything we have – apart from the house, which belonged to his father and came to him as a matter of course – he has earned himself. Hubert is one of those people who hate being given presents because they have never learned how to be grateful.

If you knew his mother you could understand why: even I, who gets all excited over a bunch of flowers, would never have wanted a present from her.

Anyway, that was Hubert's mother and my mother in law. Ferdinand's grandmother, on the other hand, must have been quite a different woman – seeing that he was fond of her and even now likes to talk about her occasionally.

I reckoned it was time I put an end to this train of thought, so I began thinking about the housekeeping money instead, and started doing complicated sums in my head. It worked, because I'm bad at mental arithmetic and had to think really hard. Next I tried to work out the dates of certain family events, going by the birth and death dates of my parents and grandparents. This is an old game I play when I'm in need of distraction. While my hands went on working I managed to calculate how long my father had been in the army, how long in the war, the year of my mother's operation, and several key dates in my grandfather's life as well. At the same time I kept a look-out for spiders' webs, which is a taxing task when I'm without my glasses.

By the time I'd finished my date calculations, my forehead was dripping with sweat and my blouse stuck fast to my skin. I'd ended up with the date of my lame uncle's first communion, and it had taken some doing. I raised my head, stretched my back, and as I was doing so, suddenly, there in the dining room where the old-fashioned dresser used to stand, I saw my mother in law. She was standing there, slim and tall, in a black woollen dress, with round her neck a gold chain that hung down to her waist. The black enamelled helmet framed her blank face with its delicate lips and thin, arched eyebrows. All my calculating efforts had been in vain. She hadn't changed at all, she still didn't smile, and she looked straight past me with a haughty stare. She reminded me a bit of the dragonflies I so often draw. I said, 'Leave it for today, will you, and you just go back where you came from.' And she slid back obediently inside my head and hid there. Sometimes it's a nuisance to have so many pictures hidden in my head, ready to pop out at any moment. People who see ghosts are probably made the same way, only they don't realise it and are therefore frightened of their own creations. It's funny to think that I am the only person left who can see Madam Magistrate so clearly. In its way her image is rather beautiful, with a cold beauty like that of a water nymph.

I began now to plan the menus for the rest of the week: a roast, noodle soup, liver with cream sauce, on Sunday roast chicken and apple fritters. Ferdinand would be coming to lunch and he loves apple fritters. He likes his food, he doesn't eat much but he enjoys it. All the more praiseworthy in him, therefore, the fact that he resists the temptation of my cooking and normally eats out in a restaurant. I wouldn't have him turning into one of those pathetic figures who can't live without Mummy's cooking.

Hubert, on the other hand, eats whatever's put before him. He's quite unspoilt on this score; his mother either couldn't or wouldn't cook, and Serafine, although she did her best, was never really much of a cook either. Ferdinand senior in fact, who relished good cuisine, never came back home at midday but always lunched out. Occasionally Hubert goes through periods of complete indifference towards eating. I don't like it when he does that because his indifference is not genuine, what it really means is: look at me, I am a high-minded, ascetic man who cares nothing for the pleasures of the table; I'm so wrapped up in my thoughts I have no time for such lowly things as eating. Then he sucks his cheeks inwards and looks not so much high-minded as downright cross, and between his eyebrows a deep furrow forms that he likes to think he inherited from his father. The furrow, though, is not genuine either, he just holds it in place with muscle power, and when he forgets about it, it immediately disappears.

While I set about dusting, Ilse suddenly came into my mind – as if she was a great novelty, as if I'd only just realised for the first time that I had a daughter. I worried about her for a couple of minutes – on a skiing holiday all sorts of things can happen – but I soon discovered that my worry was mere play acting, and I felt ashamed. No, I never really worry about Ilse, she doesn't need me to. It seems crazy but that's the way it is. I made up my mind to buy her a new smart pair of boots, and then felt ashamed again. You spend money to placate a guilty conscience, and if you don't even have that, you spend still more.

I love giving presents, partly because I love receiving them, but also, I think, because I want to buy people's affection, or else buy myself free of them for a while. Nothing is so difficult as probing one's own intentions. I get sudden insights now and again but introspection gets me nowhere: I either know or I don't. My thoughts are like a flock of birds, winging around all over the place. Sometimes a wing grazes me lightly and awakens things inside me that until then have been deep asleep – pictures that I can't summon up myself but that are suddenly there, blazing with colour. In that instant I know things I've never known before. And then I forget them again. Which is why I consider thinking a second-rate activity. This only holds good for me, though; other people may well get somewhere by thinking, I never do myself. Thinking is only helpful in small matters, matters of little importance. With anything larger it leads me straight into muddle and disaster. All the wrong decisions of my life I have arrived at after careful thought, and I go on doing this because it has been dinned into me since a child that human beings ought to think. Either I'm not a human being or else the advice was wrong: I use thought like a guide-dog, for when my eyes are closed and I can't see any pictures. Unfortunately, though, the habit I've been taught is so strong that my thoughts play havoc with me and rarely leave me in peace.

I'd clean forgotten about Ilse by now, but as I went on with my dusting a feeling of weariness came over me. It often does when I dust, probably because this activity reminds me more strongly than anything else of the futility of all human endeavour. Even the bookshelves were already covered over again with a fine grey film. I shuffled around like a very old woman, from the table to the bookshelves to the desk, and felt as if I were shrouded in a thick grey fog. Summoning up my last energies I decided to come to grips with this grime in earnest. I ran to the bathroom, filled a bucket with water, grabbed a floor cloth and knelt down and began washing the parquet. I didn't use a broom, I just crawled around on all fours and got right into every corner, the way you never can do when you're standing up. It was a terrific feeling and it chased away my thoughts completely. It's such hard work, you have to stretch out and wriggle under cupboards and move bits of furniture, and your back aches and your hands smart; for clearing the mind of intrusive thoughts, nothing works better.

By the time I'd finished there was a thick fog outside the window – a real one – but it didn't bother me one bit. If Hubert could have seen me he'd have been horrified. For a moment I wished he was here so that I could run to him and throw my arms round him and laugh or cry or at any rate do something that showed him I still loved him. But it would have rattled him badly, there's nothing he finds so disconcerting as people showing too much emotion, or what he considers to be too much emotion. I try to spare him these kinds of shock as a rule, because any little push might cause him to lose his balance, and I don't want that happening, absolutely not. Besides, I hardly ever feel like laughing or crying – it's just an idea I toy with now and again, that's all.

Now I actually did give a tiny laugh, but I broke off straight away, appalled. There was nothing to laugh about, definitely not for me: outside in the letterbox there was bound to be another present already, sitting there waiting. I decided not to worry about this for the time being, though, and to carry on with my reflections. Maybe I play these mental games with myself because I'm never quite at ease, alone in a house. In a room, yes, but, not alone in an entire house. If you are alone in a room you can always go the next door down the corridor, knock on it and ask, 'May I come in for a minute?' And the person inside says, 'Yes, my child, come on in.' So in I go and sit down on the big green sofa, and the person sits down beside me and smokes his pipe and tells me dozens of little stories that have no end and no beginning, until, after a while, I'm capable of going back to my own room again.

The person in the next door room is unfailingly my grandfather, and his place will never be taken by another. Because this is a memory image, you see, and there's nothing I can do to alter it. Who else but him would call me 'my child'? There's no way of shielding yourself from memory images, even though you know they may be harmful.

Hubert never sits on a green sofa, and he smokes no pipe, only cigarettes. He sits at his desk, and a desk is a solitary piece of furniture: impossible for two people to sit together at a desk. Hubert tells no stories either, and the ones he knows, he won't tell me – no doubt he has his reasons. The best we can do is to sit in our armchairs and tell one another about the various little things that have happened to us during the day. I am better at this than he is: I tell him what the tobacconist said to me, how many birds I counted on the balcony, and about a white cat that has recently shown up in the neighbourhood. I don't know if Hubert really needs to hear all this, but if he doesn't he could always get up and go somewhere else, and this he never does; instead he sits there listening and widening his eyes in surprise, and sometimes he even laughs, although in a hesitant way like someone who has lost the habit. The important thing though is that we sit there and recite a scene, which may not be the real scene but is a fairly good approximation of it. The real scene, alas, we never will play.

I knelt down on the floor and stared into the bucket with its dirty water. I knew that something very important had just gone through my head, indicating something bad, something very wrong in my make up: nobody and nothing should ever be a replacement for something or somebody else. From my nineteenth year onwards I had used people for the simple purpose of being able to go on dreaming my childhood dreams undisturbed, and in so doing I had committed countless crimes. This was a terrifying thought and I did my best to forget it straight away.

By now I was truly exhausted. I carried the bucket into the bathroom and poured its contents down the drain. Then I rinsed it out as if the fate of the world depended on its cleanliness. This was in order to rid myself immediately of the insight I had just had. The first part of my housework was now complete. Almost, that is: I still had to beat the carpets. Not all of them, only those in the living room; to do all of them would have been beyond me.

The garden is rather small and run-down and is surrounded by a box hedge which has an unfortunate cemetery smell about it. I'd much rather have hornbeam, but who would plant it for me? Nothing old is ever dug out here and nothing new is planted. The garden knows it is unloved and wilts away in consequence, nothing grows properly in it, the box is the only real spot of green. The lawn is patchy and yellowing, the roses revert to wild and each year bear smaller flowers, and they suffer from everything roses can possibly suffer from. In one corner there's a table, to which a couple of chairs get added in the summer, and behind it grows a pear tree whose fruit tastes of turnips and rots on the bough before it even ripens. And I do nothing for this poor, ailing garden, I don't know why. Once I put in a couple of peonies but they didn't flourish either; they went dry and yellow and I dug them out again with a kind of grim satisfaction. Peonies are not meant to bloom here, they belong in quite a different garden, one that only exists inside my head. There, in that timeless dimension, their red petals blaze and the ants run up and down their stalks for ever.

I stopped my carpet beating and stood there, just getting my breath back, and watched the sun trying desperately for the umpteenth time to penetrate the fog. It still couldn't make it. My eyes were smarting, and I loosened my hold on all the fond images from the past – the geraniums, the viburnum bushes, the dahlias and the guelder roses – and let them fade away. Then I took firm hold of the carpet and dragged it back inside the house. With that my morning was really and truly over. I washed my hands and face in the bathroom and told myself I'd made a good job of things, and was forced to recognise that, no matter how much I loathed it, this kind of work was necessary to me. Next I went to the letterbox, took out the yellow envelope and carried it up to the loft. I was too tired to bother about it much and merely tucked it away in a drawer under a block of sketching paper. After this I went back down to the kitchen, poured myself a glass of milk and made a sandwich. Hubert was miles away from me and probably lunching at that very moment with Dr Melichar, chewing his cud contentedly the way I was mine; we could have been twins.

I didn't sit down because then I'd have to get up again, and at my present stage of tiredness this was impossible. The milk didn't taste of milk but at least it was nice and cold; the sandwich I couldn't eat at all. The morsel I had bitten off seemed to get bigger and bigger in my mouth, and I couldn't swallow it so I spat it out. Then I noticed that the bread knife was lying with its blade pointing upwards, and I turned it quickly downwards again, because if you leave it that way the souls in purgatory are forced to ride on it. I don't recall who told it to me, but this superstition has haunted me since childhood: it's not that I believe in souls in purgatory, it's just the thought of them riding on knives that I can't bear.

The idea of having rescued these poor creatures afforded me a certain feeling of satisfaction, but at the same time I realised how unspeakably tired I was on this particular Wednesday. Could it be I was feeling my age? Hubert told me once I ought to engage a helper, but I refused, and since then he seems to have forgotten the matter. He's never mentioned it since, at any rate, and I approve of this: it would never cross my mind to ask him how he runs his office, or whether he's a good lawyer or a bad one, or whether he should increase his staff. There's no way married people can help each other on such matters. Sometimes, very rarely, he tells me about a case of his, and I listen carefully, strangely moved by this foreign world in which he spends his days; and not only days but years – his entire life. Then I pay him back by inviting him up to the loft to look at my drawings. He likes everything I draw, partly because it's I who have drawn it and partly because he likes the idea of my having what he considers a hobby. He must never find out that it isn't a hobby, although he has probably suspected this for a long time: married couples know a lot about each other without having to put everything in words.

After exchanges like these we keep out of each other's way for a while. But they happen so seldom we don't really feel the need to discuss them. Hubert just takes to his desk; Ilse goes her own way as per usual; and I spend more time in the loft. In this way we compensate for the overdose of intimacy. Ilse has a habit of studying to the sound of rock music, which makes her father deeply suspicious about what she's up to, but he can't forbid it because she keeps the volume down. I don't give much thought to the matter: I reckon you can easily learn things to the sound of rock music when you're made the way Ilse is. It's not for me to doubt her word. She often has friends in, too, because her room is big and there's plenty of space. When she does, I prepare a snack for them, and leave it in the kitchen for her to come and fetch. I like the idea of these girls being there, and of Ilse being popular with them and having a world of her own. It's nice for her to have friends she can laugh with. What they talk about, I haven't a clue. They look quite different from how girls did in my day – tall, most of them, and voluptuous and without a care in the world. Ilse herself is already taller than me and can't fit into my clothes. I can see no trace in her of that curiosity we used to have, either. She seems to know everything and to take it all for granted – the only things that interest her appear to be her records, her sewing (which is rather unexpected), and her soft toys, of which she has a large collection, scattered all over the place. It's all very odd, I can't really make it out. Her marks at school are always good – she has inherited her father's memory, which makes things easy for her – but she seems to regard learning as a necessary evil. What she will end up doing, I have no idea.

Nor can I speak about this to Hubert, because for him she is still a child who plays with furry animals and who just happens by chance to look like a woman. It would upset him to have to think about her femininity, let alone talk about it. Sometimes I have the feeling that in his heart of hearts he'd like her to go on sitting in her room forever, doing homework and playing records, so that nothing during his lifetime will have to change. I think it surprises him as much as it does me that this young woman we know so little about, is our own daughter. Of course we don't know much about Ferdinand either, but in his case it is different, our relationship to him is more like the relationship that binds us to each other. Ferdinand is technically younger than we are, but he belongs with us because he sprang from that early period of our lives when things were not grey but beautiful and brightly coloured. You can talk to him about most things like a grownup – which is what he is – but he never mentions his private life to us. Hubert has sometimes seen him in town in the company of a young woman who he says looks a bit older than Ferdinand, and whom he describes as 'striking'. I doubt I shall ever set eyes on her.

All this I find a bit unsettling. People who can't run their own lives properly shouldn't meddle in those of others. In reality I know nothing at all about these things: even today I feel that everything that happens between men and women is strange and, when looked at objectively, almost inexplicable. It's just that, since it goes on all the time, we have got used to it and nobody gives it a thought.

My own early experiences are vague in my memory. I only know it used to make a big impression on me when a man turned out to have very warm hands. A bit as if those years I spent in this city as a young woman were all part of one long wartime winter, during which I latched onto warmth wherever I could find it. Certain young men I met then didn't suffer the cold, and they acted on me like wonderful electric stoves: even if I can't recall their faces I am grateful to them on this account.

If this is all I remember in my own case, how could I ever presume to understand that of other people? Who can tell what reasons they have for doing things or not doing them?

A long time ago, during the holidays I spent in the country when my grandfather was still alive, I used to meet up at night with a young man I'd known ever since I was a child. We would go hedgehog hunting together, and now and again we would stop and kiss – it seemed to be part of the proceedings. In fact I was more taken up with the adventure and the hedgehogs. They rustled around in the undergrowth, stomping heavily, and were easy to find. When you caught one it would pass on to you all its fleas and then trot off again into the bushes. The meadows smelt of hay, and at intervals a pear would suddenly fall off a tree and onto the ground. The noise rang loud in the still night air, and we would cling to one another in fright.

The telephone rang and, befuddled, I picked up the receiver. On the line was the Nice Lady, asking if she could come and visit me on Friday. There is no denying the requests of nice ladies of her ilk: we exchanged a few civil words and I hung up again. Her visit didn't fit in with my plans at all but on the telephone I am always overridden. The Nice Lady has a registered name and surname but it never comes to mind and one day I'm bound to forget it altogether: I'm not much good with names. The Nice Lady herself, for that matter, only comes to mind when she calls me up, and this happens roughly three times a year. She is an extraordinary creature. When Ilse was born she and I shared a room for ten days in the same nursing home, and since then she has always paid me regular visits. We have nothing in common bar the fact that we gave birth to a child at the same time, but to her this seems to be link enough.

I still hadn't sat down for a second, and my knees now started shaking. I poured out another glass of milk, finally seated myself at the kitchen table and started leafing through the newspaper. Suddenly I felt very cold. Hardly surprising, when I'd sweated so hard from all that carpet beating and hadn't yet changed my clothes. I had the feeling I'd never be able to stand up again. I could, of course, go and lie down on my bed – there was nothing to stop me – but it would have interfered with my system and I dismissed the thought immediately.

I place a lot of importance on my bed. It's long and it's wide, and its quilt is deliciously soft and warm. Even as a child I liked going to bed. I looked on it as a comfortable burrow that I could crawl into after a day of cares. And in those days, when my parents were still alive, nearly every day was a day of cares. When I get into bed I read for about ten minutes, then I pull the bedclothes round my ears and give myself up entirely to the pleasure of slowly switching off. I dream a lot, and in my dreams there is still a certainty of everything turning out right, a pinch of hope that I can no longer experience in waking life. Small wonder I like my bed so much.

It worries me, the fact that Hubert so dislikes going to sleep. His eyes keep shutting, but there he sits, in front of the television. Sometimes he drinks coffee in order to be able to go on working at his desk. It doesn't look much like working to me – he just sits there for ages, staring straight in front of him, which is enough to give anyone insomnia. He says bed puts him in mind of a coffin, and that's why he doesn't like it. He's always afraid of missing out on something, but on what I have no idea. I really don't understand him. He claims he never dreams – probably he just forgets his dreams the moment he wakes up. It sometimes helps if I talk to him about silly little things I've been doing during the day – in which case he can drop off quite suddenly, but it doesn't usually happen until I'm right on the brink of sleep myself. I hear him moving around in the bed; I'd like to say something but I can't; and then it's too late, I'm gone, into the land of dreams where hope still flourishes. Yes, it really troubles me that Hubert doesn't appreciate sleep. I myself don't sleep as well as I used to. Round about four a.m. I wake up, to find myself a completely different person. This scares me because the four o'clock me is an alien, destructive being, out to kill me.

I was getting colder and colder. I got up and rinsed the milk glass. The telephone rang: a wrong number. I put on a sweater and went out on the veranda to clean it up a bit. The veranda is built of wood, and I'm very fond of it. The wood is old and grey and has a silky shine to it when it catches the light. Hubert wanted to have it pulled down but I dissuaded him. In the summer it is my little sun house – I greatly prefer sitting there to sitting in the garden. In passing I sometimes stroke my finger along the surface of its slats – there is something so nice about touching old wood.

I went on with my housework until half past four, by which time I was through for the day so I had a wash, changed, and went out to do some shopping. Hubert got back shortly after six – on Dr Melichar days he is always home a little earlier than usual. He looked relaxed and his eyes sparkled. I was aching all over but I was pleased to see him in such good form. God bless Dr Melichar, whoever he may be. I figure he must be a bit of a character, or he wouldn't amuse Hubert the way he does.

Supper was a lively meal and we finished off a bottle of red wine between us. I didn't drink much but my head spun a little, even though it remained crystal clear. Hubert didn't watch television that evening but read an art book instead that had come with the morning post. The post had brought something for me as well, so when I saw Hubert so comfortably settled, up I went to the loft. Not to draw – there was no question of that – but to do my duty. This time I didn't walk up and down while I read but sat down at the desk. I'm not used to drinking, and I felt very strange, as if my head, instead of resting firmly on my shoulders, was hovering in the air, light and empty, a few inches above them.

April 2nd

The snow has gone and so has the frost, whose crisp crunching sound I couldn't hear. In March it thawed. The snow turned bluish and matt, and one morning the southern side of the meadows lay there, uncovered. Browny yellowy blades of grass poked up, freed from their winter burden, and a little later the first flowers began to appear: liverwort and clover. No, just liverwort to begin with. I tried painting some but couldn't get the right blue. It is too pretty to paint; I'm not up to the task.

March was not a very nice month, all things considered: the thaw, and all the unrest that I couldn't hear, only see, I found unsettling.

I can see the melted snow overflowing the banks of the stream, and can imagine to myself the splashing, gurgling noises that it makes. But then I grow tired of imagining noises, and even in my dreams all is silent. The world is becoming more and more mute, and I am growing more and more isolated. This is bad for me, I know, but there's nothing I can do about it. I still haven't gone to the village. The gamekeeper brings me everything I need, and I need less and less as time goes on. It costs me increasing effort to get up in the morning, wash, put on clean clothes, and do the tiny amount of housework that is necessary. Every movement I make tires me. Now and again I cut my hair with a pair of paper shears, but only when it reaches my shoulders and begins to get in my way. I hold it back with an Alice band. I've given up using lipstick and my mouth is pale, sometimes almost white.

I've taken to roaming the woods. The gamekeeper doesn't like me doing this. He wrote a note, 'Don't stray far! Dangerous!' 'Why?' I asked. He gave me a cold, angry look. 'Unsavoury types in the district,' he wrote, 'I am responsible for your safety.' At that I had to laugh. It must have sounded like the cawing of a raven or the shriek of a magpie, because he tore the note out of my hand and crammed it in the stove. Then he left, slamming the door behind him – I could feel the draught on my cheek. I put on my walking shoes and went straight out into the wood. The wood that comes right down to the back of the house and cloaks the taller of my two gaolers, the mountain.

I have a theory that mountains don't like standing too close to one another, but that each of them would prefer to rear up alone in the middle of a wide plain. They wouldn't feel lonely on this account, either: now and again an eagle would fly over and bring a bit of earth and grass from another mountain in its beak, and, for a big mountain, this would be comfort enough and would warm its stone heart in a very pleasant way. It would be nice to be a mountain, but I am not one, I am still just a humble and bewildered mole cricket.

I tried to paint a bird, an Alpine finch, but it came to nothing: it looked pretty but entirely alone, as if it were the only bird of its kind in the whole world. Once, shortly after I'd met Hubert, I drew a starling that looked almost happy and seemed to be listening to something. I packed it away in a suitcase and left it with some friends in the country where I thought it would be safe, but the house was hit by a bomb. In the case, which was very big, there was my trousseau, which my grandfather had given me, a silver cutlery service for six, some good bits of china, and the starling. I didn't mind about the other things but the loss of the starling I do mind. Material possessions meant little to me, but I'm pretty sure I'll never be able to draw a starling like that again, how could I?

Hubert writes that he has found rooms for his office and is in the process of furnishing them. The apartment, however, has been snapped up by another person who was prepared to pay higher rent, but he already has something else in view. Ferdinand is fine, he sends kisses and a little photograph. It can't be true about the kisses – Ferdinand will have long since forgotten me, at most he will remember me as someone out of a fairy story. He is four years old now. I put the photograph away immediately.

Every day I go walking in the woods. If I walk fast enough I have to worry about not tripping over roots, and this keeps me occupied and stops me from thinking. I go right up to the ridge of the mountain and down the other side until I come to a small lake into which the torrent of the Prusch pours. There is another much easier way of reaching this lake but I prefer the hard one: easy ways are not for me. I haven't yet met up with any of the gamekeeper's unsavoury types, only a couple of foresters and, by the lake itself, the odd fisherman. There are two small wooden huts on its shore, set far apart, I imagine they are lived in in the summer and belong to city folk.

The water of the lake is a dark green colour and looks very cold. In several parts it's almost black, which must mean it's deep. You probably can't swim there even in summer. I stand on the shore and watch the fish: it's hard to believe how they can survive the endless cold but they look very healthy and lively. I talk to them. I say, 'Keep away from the shore so that no one can see you'. I know there's no way they'll understand me but I talk to them just the same. It would seem that human beings have to talk if they don't want to lose their wits entirely. Maybe I've lost mine already without realising it. Sometimes I see eyes looking out at me from the undergrowth – little woodland animals staring at me the same way that I stare at the fishes. All of us close, and none of us knowing anything about the other.

June 26th

I haven't written anything for nearly three months. Spring is harder to endure than winter. Hubert wanted to come for Easter but I begged him to stay away. What's the point of our tormenting each other? He's so conscientious that I can only stop him coming by telling him clearly in writing that I don't want him here and that his visit would be bad for me. He will do anything as long as it's for my good. I can imagine how he suffers from the relief that my letters must bring him. It gives me no pleasure to imagine it, and not because I'm noble minded but because anything that hurts him is bound to hurt me as well. It has always been like this. Doubtless he'll get the apartment, but it will never be my home. What good is a deaf wife to a young lawyer, what good would she be to any husband? And what kind of a mother could I ever be to little Ferdinand? It doesn't bear thinking about. For the time being it's enough that Hubert pays my keep. But one day that, too, will stop. I still get commissions to illustrate children's books and the like; the last one was for butterflies – pretty butterflies in the conventional style that the publishers wanted from me. One day I'll stop being a financial burden to Hubert, but I'll go on being a burden to him in other ways for as long as we live.

We were so happy together – a little incredulous and a little unsure of ourselves still, but that could have been remedied. Or perhaps not. It's possible that we wouldn't have been able to stand the excessive closeness for long and that we would have reverted to our original positions: me going back to my drawing, and he to his friends, whom he treated like court jesters. We shall never know. I hope for him he finds another wife, or at least some more cheerful jesters.

I no longer know what it feels like to be touched by him. All I can remember is that little Ferdinand always had very hot hands and that he smelt delicious, even when he wasn't freshly washed. Grownups don't smell as nice as children. I haven't seen one child since I've been here, and I'm glad I haven't.

In May the winter suddenly returned, and I put aside the butterflies and went back to the Roman Empire. The weather turned cold, and it snowed. Day by day the gamekeeper seemed to get worse tempered, and once he hit his dog in a particularly cruel fashion. I saw him from the window: the dog howled, and it howled silently, and it was so terrible that I crawled into my bed and wept. It's possible I howled as loud as the dog did. I thought I would choke. Towards evening the dog crawled back to the house on its belly, and a little later I saw it follow its master into the woods, wagging its tail. It limped slightly but it looked happy. I wanted to kill both of them. Maybe the dog is better off, really, than the gamekeeper. Yes, I reckon it is.

On that evening something went wrong inside me, and I spent two days in bed, my face turned to the wall. I can't remember what I thought about during this time, but I know it was horrible.

The third morning the gamekeeper prised the key out of the lock and opened it with a skeleton key. 'Go away,' I yelled at him. He scribbled a note: 'I am responsible for you. Shall I fetch a doctor?' 'No,' I said faintly. 'Leave me alone, then I'll get up.' He left, taking the note and the key with him. Round about midday I crawled out of bed. It was icy cold in the room and I felt very weak and saw everything double. The gamekeeper must have heard me because he came up, lit the stove, and then brought me a bowl of soup – thick, grey, mealy liquid. I was perched in the leather chair and I couldn't hold the spoon, so the gamekeeper fed me. The soup tasted delicious.

Why shouldn't I take soup from him? Who am I to make such a fuss? His eyes were as expressionless as always, but they had a worried look. He doesn't want me to die because he needs the money. Or maybe he was really concerned for me, I won't rule it out entirely.

This happened sometime in May. Some days are as long as weeks, and some weeks fly by like a day. When I see the gamekeeper going off to church in his best suit I know it is Sunday. If I miss seeing him like this, as I often do, then I don't know what day it is. Every so often he brings me a newspaper. I read everything that's in it but it doesn't interest me at all; I use the pages for lighting the fire.

Since I didn't want to be fed by the gamekeeper a second time I started living again. By which I mean that I got up when it was light, did my work, and then went out into the woods. Later on I sat in the chair and read about the rise and fall of the Roman Empire. Every day I put out food for the birds on the window sill, and occasionally I did a bit of drawing. But all this I did in order not to fall ill again and be dependent on the gamekeeper. I don't want to see that strange look in his eyes any more, nor do I want things to get to the point where even he has to pity me.

July 4th

For some days now things have been better. I'm out in the woods a lot, and sometimes I have a feeling inside me of still being young and alive. There's a smell of hay in the air, and it's a smell I've always found bracing.

Hubert writes that he's still looking out for an apartment. He asks me to be patient. He writes as though it were a foregone conclusion that one day he will come and fetch me and we will carry on our life together as if nothing had happened. Does he think that the moment I cross the threshold of our new dwelling I will automatically start hearing again, or what? I don't know why he clings to this fiction, or what purpose it is meant to serve. Maybe when I'm not there he can think of me as being quite normal, just away on a voyage or something. Hubert is frightened of old and ill and ugly people; he daren't tell himself the truth. In sending me away and betraying me he has remained true to himself. And now I've written it down – the thing that up till now I haven't dared write or even think: sending me away and betraying me. Even the gamekeeper feels responsible for me, but Hubert, who would never beat a dog, has betrayed me. He must feel dreadful about it. If he ever got that apartment he would have to go on furnishing it for years, because the woman to whom he writes those (admittedly few but very caring) letters exists by now only in his head.

I wish he didn't have to feel guilty. If you want to stay alive you have to be capable of betrayal, and you have to accustom yourself to this fact the way you would accustom yourself to having bow legs or knock knees. But Hubert will never accustom himself.

Today I lay on the grassy meadow and closed my eyes. The sun shone on my face and I felt sleepy. And then I woke up because I felt someone observing me. The cat was sitting beside me, staring at me with her yellow eyes; I could tell something was passing through her head. I said something to her softly – at least I hoped it was softly – and she sprang back in fright: to her, human speech is just a prologue to violent action. So I kept quiet again, and she calmed down. It is so long since I stroked anything or anyone that I felt an urge to stroke her, and I stretched out my hand. At this she gave a great leap and went and hid behind a bush. Better that way, better that she never learns how nice it is to be stroked; it might turn her clever cat's head for her and make her lose all her cunning. Better that she stays free and brave and full of hate against her tormentors: only hatred and cunning can keep her alive. 'Trust no humans, cat,' I told her, 'they only want to hurt you and kill your kittens. Live for yourself, cat. One day they'll catch you and sell your skin, but it's not so bad to be killed by an enemy as it is by a friend. Now get that into your pretty head and chew on it.'

She poked her head out from behind the bush, and in the midday sun her eyes shone red. My hand itched to caress her soft fur, but I closed my eyes and didn't move.

August 6th

Hubert seems to have grasped that it is better not to come here on holiday, bringing little Ferdinand with him. I told him it would be much too rough here for a child, and he agrees. I'm glad his guilty conscience isn't strong enough to lead him into making mistakes. It would definitely be bad for Ferdinand to see me. I've asked Hubert to refrain from coming here himself until the apartment is ready, I said I couldn't bear the strain. This correspondence is sad for both of us, although an outsider might find it funny. And sometimes I feel such an outsider myself that I, too, find it funny. Anyone would become an outsider, living here for any length of time. Ferdinand is getting on well, Hubert writes, and I have no trouble believing it: he was always a favourite with my mother in law, and she's bound to spoil him far more than I ever did.

There are other reasons, too, why I don't want Hubert to come. I might scream, for example, every time he touched me, and this would be very upsetting for both of us – particularly since I don't know what my screams sound like. I imagine they sound awful and would scare Hubert to bits.

Nowadays I often think about my parents. They managed to die of tuberculosis without making any great fuss. They sent me away as soon as they could, and they never kissed me and hardly ever touched me either. Maybe it hurt them to see that I was only really comfortable with my grandfather and not with them. I never thought about these things before, and now it is too late: all those who could throw any light on the matter are dead. I was very hungry for affection when I was a child, I used to stroke every dog and cat I could get hold of, and when there were none around I would stroke trees and stones instead. Hungry? I must have been starved. But on the other hand I didn't like being held close myself, and being kissed and stroked by someone else, and I was glad my grandfather didn't go in for such things. He used to look at me, and I knew he loved me, and sometimes we would walk hand in hand together through the fields, but it went no further than that.

Hubert was very demonstrative at the start of our marriage. It used to scare me slightly: I had an attack of angina once, as a child, and it made me very thirsty, but when I was given water, I couldn't swallow. I hope he never noticed I was scared. I was perfectly happy, as happy as a grownup person can be. This is why I find it so hard now to keep my distance from the cat. I can no longer picture to myself what Hubert's face looks like, and this is so painful that I have stopped trying.

Yesterday I bathed in the lake. It was as if I was cut in two separate pieces. Afterwards I lay on the grass and shivered. The water is murderously cold. It is uncanny, swimming, when you can't hear the soft splashing noise of your dive. What sort of a place is this, I wonder, where even in August the water is so cold it stings?

September 7th

I'm glad the summer is coming to an end. A summer of deathly calm. Storms that I can only see, not hear; rain drumming down in silence; an unheard wind tearing at my hair; a chorus of birds, not sung for my ears; a pack of hounds running past me in full cry, making not a sound. It is like the still world of an old painting. Things will be better in winter, when I can curl up in my leather chair and read and draw. Certainly it will hurt less. I shall slowly freeze to death without even noticing.

The gamekeeper has found himself a lady friend. She visits him almost every evening – a middle aged woman, slim but with heavy, floppy breasts. She is missing two front teeth, and her eyes are as colourless as his are. As soon as it starts to get dark she disappears into the house. It could be that he beats her like he does his dog: I have no way of knowing what goes on in the room below mine. When we meet she gives me a sideways glance, pert and obsequious at the same time. I won't betray her secret, if it is a secret at all.

I have nearly made up my mind now to go to the village. Once I was on the point of setting out, but then I saw the houses in the distance and turned back again and slid my shopping note under the gamekeeper's door. I missed the opportunity. I should have gone there from the start; people would have been used to me by now. It's too late now; it's too late for everything.

I am drawing a magpie, a beautiful shiny creature. It looks more solitary than any bird I've ever drawn, and cold and slightly malicious on top of it. I don't like this magpie but it has come out very well. I wouldn't like to have it hanging in my room, I am scared of it.

October 15th

Today I went to a deserted mountain farmstead. The gamekeeper doesn't care anymore where I go. He seems to have grasped that his 'I am responsible for you' notes make no impression on me. It is very lonely up there and it suits me well. On my way down I came across a place where cranberries grow. They weren't quite red yet because they were still unripe, and they looked like the beads of a coral necklace. I ate a handful: they are indescribably bitter and taste of tannic acid.

As I neared the lake I saw a man sitting outside one of the wooden shacks, staring into the water. At least that is what I imagine he was doing: all I could see of him was his back and the nape of his neck, which was covered with short, copper-coloured curls. He turned round and said something to me. I tried to form my words clearly and said, 'I am deaf. If you want to say anything to me you must put it down in writing.' He stared at me for a moment, then he seemed to think of something, and went and fetched a biro and a piece of paper out of his jacket pocket and wrote: 'You really can't hear anything at all?' I nodded. This seemed to please him. At any rate he invited me – in writing, naturally – to have a glass of lemonade. I could tell it wasn't done out of pity, so I accepted. It seemed a great adventure, to drink a glass of lemonade with another human being. The man has a very unusual face, white-complexioned and broad, and his eyes are remarkably wide-set and are as clear as water. His mouth is large and pale, with healthy teeth, stained by tobacco. What strikes you most is the wide-set eyes and the copper coloured hair. The overall impression is one of ugliness rather than handsomeness, and there is something scary about him too.

112

But there you are, I can't be choosy about finding someone willing to drink lemonade with me and talk. Yes, talk: he seemed actually to want to talk to me, and to be pleased by the fact that I cannot hear. He has the look of a man who is totally alone but who cannot bear solitude. At first he proceeded very carefully, studying me hard, but once he realised I truly couldn't hear or even lip-read he got into his stride and paid me no more attention. I think he might even have shouted – that is what it looked like, anyway. Since I found it rather repugnant to watch him I ended up by staring at the lake instead. After a while I turned round again and saw that something terrible had happened to his face. It had gone all shapeless and runny; it was hardly a face any more. His hair was stuck to his forehead, and little rivulets of sweat ran down into his collar. He smelt tangy and unpleasant. I got up and said, 'Thank you for the lemonade; it's time for me to go now.' For a second I thought he was going to keep me there by force, but then he regained control of himself and wrote down something else on the scrap of paper. His hand was shaking so hard I could hardly read the words, despite their being written in capital letters.

It's a strange business altogether. It turns out that he wants me to go and visit him as often as possible, and let him talk to me. He looked so wild and despairing that I did my best to smile. 'Tomorrow,' I told him. Then I turned and went without looking back, but I had a feeling that he stood there watching me until he could see me no longer.

In the meantime I have thought the matter over. I have decided the man is not mad, even though eyes like that can't belong to a completely normal person. I think he has an un-confessable secret that is weighing on him. It would be safer to tell it to a dog, or even to a tree, but he probably doesn't have much imagination and needs a dummy in human shape to talk to. The gamekeeper would probably write a note saying, 'He might be a murder. I am responsible for you.' But even if the man were a murderer, he's not going to murder me, because he needs me.

It's a curious feeling, to be needed by someone again after such a long time. I shall definitely go. Maybe I can get used to the man's face and smell. Extraordinary: somebody needs me. Well, not me personally, just my physical presence. That lemonade tasted sticky and horrid. I can no longer recall the taste of the cranberries, and that is a shame.

I screwed the pages I had read into a ball and took them down to the cellar. Then I stood by and watched them burn. My hand-writing has altered a lot since those days: it is not so sloping, and the capitals are formed differently, they no longer have that school-taught look about them. That was all that came into my mind at that moment.

My head was back tight on my shoulders again, but I felt very tired and wished the week was over. I sat down on the beer crate, my head in my hands, and waited until all the pages were reduced to ashes.

Hubert was in the living room, turning on the television. I sat down beside him on the sofa and must have fallen asleep immediately. When I woke up, my head was resting on his shoulder, and he told me I had slept for a whole hour. He poured me out a glass of brandy and I noticed he had already drunk some himself. This was unusual for us. As a rule Hubert only drinks when he's tensed up about something, never when he's depressed, and I only drink to keep him company.

The programme hadn't finished yet, but Hubert switched the television off and we went up to bed together. Things went the way they always do when alcohol rids him of his inhibitions. Afterwards he went straight to sleep, and I lay awake for a while: I had already slept an hour in front of the television.

Thursday

On Thursday Hubert had a court hearing so I decided to go to the hairdresser. After a cleaning day I like having my hair done, it needs it, it gets so dull and dusty. It was nice, too, not having to hurry, there is nothing I dislike more than having to hurry.

During the night the wind had changed to south, and I convinced myself that I had foreseen the change yesterday, before it happened. There was a blue sky, and it was unnaturally warm. I don't mind a south wind; it's only the north wind that bothers me. It makes me tired and ill, and I ache all over and really feel my age. The south wind, on the contrary, perks me up and makes me cheerful and alert. I can see better and hear better and my sense of smell is keener than normal. By the time evening comes I am usually exhausted, but I am still wide awake and can't get to sleep without a sleeping pill. It is a misery not being able to sleep when you share a bed with someone: I daren't read or move much for fear of waking Hubert. If I can't get off to sleep at all I slip out of the room and go up to the loft where I read for a bit or look through my old drawings. And that, of course, wakes me up even more. Eventually I lie down on the sofa, toss around for a while, and finally fall asleep.

As a matter of fact I would like to use the loft as my bedroom now and again, but Hubert won't hear of it. I don't know why this suggestion should upset him so badly, but it clearly does. So much so that I hardly dare mention it. It is terrible when I have a cold. Why Hubert should insist on sleeping beside a woman who sneezes every other minute, I can't think. Every time I cough or blow my nose he gives a faint, defeated sigh. There is nothing worse than having to be discreet about blowing your nose – as a method it simply doesn't work. After each sigh I hate him for a couple of minutes. Why on earth doesn't he just let me go up to the loft on my own and do to my nose whatever I like? At the very least, he should omit the sighing. These sighs are illogical, worse, they are blackmail; they make me feel guilty when there is no cause for guilt whatsoever.

Regularly, every spring and every autumn, I get a cold, and then the torment starts. True, my colds only go on for about a week, but they are extremely heavy while they last, so that a week seems a long time. I feel dreadful, and totally out of sympathy with my own body; and when I see Hubert sitting there, pale and hollow-eyed, in front of his frugal breakfast, I could hit him over the head with a loaf. I don't actually do so, of course, but I'd like to see his reaction if I did. At my first sneeze, I say, 'I think it might be better if I slept in the loft tonight.' Hubert puts on his *pater familias* face and says, 'No, you will stay put. The loft is draughty, and one of the springs of the day-bed is broken. Do you take me for Bluebeard, that at the first sign of a cold I send my wife to sleep in a freezing loft?' But the loft is actually no draughtier than any other part of the house, and the broken spring doesn't bother me one bit. It's ridiculous that Hubert can't bear to be separated from me for any length of time. If I wanted to go on a trip on my own he would consider it tantamount to a betrayal. This stirs up loft-thoughts that are unworthy of me. Has he really forgotten the past, or is he trying to make amends for it? Is he carrying out a lifelong penance, or does he love me more than he did then? I shall never know, and it doesn't matter much either way, seeing that I have no intention of ever travelling on my own. Hubert is good at keeping his own counsel. I think he finds motives for all his behaviour and builds them into a rational edifice that on no account must fall. It must be hard work. I shouldn't hate him when he sighs, not for a single minute, but I do.

I pottered around for a while, and it was nine before I left the house. A new envelope was lying in the post-box but I didn't bother to take it back inside. The south wind was making my head clear, and it seemed to me that I knew a lot of things – things that I would have preferred not to know. I suppressed these loft-thoughts smartly, and it occurred to me it was not really the right kind of day for a visit to the hairdresser. The south wind makes my hair hard to handle: it goes electric and sticks out in all directions like cat's fur. But Lisa would take care of that.

Lisa is my hairdresser, and I am a little bit in love with her. She is the most ravishing being you can imagine. She has long, dark hair, looped back into a knot, skin the colour of palest milky coffee, a small, full mouth, and long, dark, slanting eyes with a very sweet expression. I could look at her for hours on end: she is the essence of femininity. Everything about her is attractive – her voice, the way she moves, and the grace and tranquillity that she irradiates. It is not that she is plump exactly – there's not a trace of fat about her – but she is dainty and well-rounded. I suppose she must have bones like everyone else, but you can't see them, and that I like. I have never once seen her lose her temper. Her smile fills the little salon with a sense of peace, and transforms it into a temple where, in many little secret rituals, sacrifice is offered at the shrine of a very ancient goddess.

Lisa works all day in the salon, but in the evenings she takes care of her husband and daughter, cooks food for the next day, washes and irons and is never in bed before eleven. She didn't tell me that herself but I can imagine it. On Mondays she does her housework, and Sundays she dedicates entirely to her family. Despite this her hands are soft and smooth without so much as a chipped nail. I have been marvelling over her now for three years. How does she manage it? How does she pull it off? And what goes through her head, I wonder? Sometimes I think, not a great deal, and that is what makes her so perfect. There is not a line to spoil the smoothness of her forehead. And yet she must be clever, it is simply that it doesn't show. And that is another nice thing about her. Everything she says is right and fitting, although she never utters a sentence that you couldn't find in any women's magazine. And on top of it all she has a magician's memory. Of all the women I know, she is the only one who has tried every singe brand of wash powder. She knows how to lay a table properly – something that always causes me headaches. And she knows what hat to wear with what dress, and what shoes would look right with it, and what shaped handbag. All things that I would find intolerably boring if they didn't come from Lisa, but in her pretty mouth they sound like the height of wisdom, and make me feel inadequate and foolish.

By nature, however, Lisa is not a talkative person, and certain topics she avoids altogether. She never mentions illness, for example, or politics. The only political remark I have ever heard her make is that she abhors excess in any sphere, and that too is right and fitting. Mostly, she goes about her work in silence; occasionally she lifts an eyebrow, or a smile plays about the corners of her mouth. She too must have her secrets, but she keeps them to herself. It is concession enough that her pretty hands are there to busy themselves about her clients' unlovely heads, always with the same dose of goodwill. Never the scratch of a nail on their scalps, never a roller pinned too tightly; and when they are under the dryer, around she goes like a benevolent deity, regulating the temperature, bringing magazines, and dispensing smiles for all. If someone lights up a cigarette, all she has to do is wrinkle her little nose ever so slightly, and the evildoer immediately stubs the cigarette out – she has trained us that well. On her feet she wears grey sling-back, peep-toe shoes that are in fact hideous, but they lend her a motherly aspect, and that is somehow right and suitable too.

Lisa's husband looks as if he might be a bit thick, but he is very well groomed and well fed. I can't quite see what she sees in him, but it's probably just the fact that he is her husband. Although this is only idle speculation because I don't really know anything about him. The little girl takes after her father and is quiet and well behaved. She has no look of Lisa at all, and this is a shame, but Lisa herself doesn't appear to mind. Her husband is a radio technician and earns good money. Lisa earns well too, so the family has a car and all the latest gadgets that you're meant to have nowadays – many more than I own myself. They go on a skiing holiday each winter, and in summer they go to the Adriatic, and all three of them are beautifully turned out. That is Lisa's world, about which I know nothing, and which would seem to me unbearable were it not inhabited by Lisa.

Today I had to wait a little. Lisa was busy with the sky-blue hair of an elderly lady who was beaming at herself, enraptured, in the mirror. This enabled me to observe Lisa at my leisure, first full-face and then in profile. An almost touching sight, this profile, with the neat little nose, if anything a trifle on the small side, and the slightly pouting under-lip. I tried to draw her profile once – from memory, naturally – but nothing came of it. Lisa is a far cry from insects, birds and lizards. I can't even draw hares properly, let alone cats. That is, I can draw them all right, but they look different from how they really are: some important element is missing. It is odd that my talent should be so limited: under the strokes of my pencil Lisa's face would turn into a vapid, empty mask.

Now she had taken leave of the blue-haired lady and came to fetch me. She always washes my hair herself – a privilege she doesn't grant to everyone. I don't delude myself that Lisa particularly likes me, it is simply that she finds me more tractable than her other clients because I appreciate everything she does. I leaned my head backwards until it rested on the rim of the basin and delivered myself into her gentle, capable hands.

I used to loathe going to the hairdresser's. I don't like strange hands taking hold of me, and I especially don't like it when they pull my hair. With Lisa it is different. Her hands are not strange hands; in fact they are so familiar that I sometimes think they must have held me once before, a long time ago.

While she was setting my hair I stole a glance in the mirror at Lisa's face, bent over her task. Why is it that I cannot draw this face? With me she knows she can relax, I hardly ever talk. I was filled with a sense of gratitude. Lisa was like a young girl playing,

119

and at the same time like a mother, bent over her child. And I was the child. It was nice to know so little about her, to know that I would never come face to face with the real Lisa. Now she must be about twenty-seven. As soon as she begins to change I will have to find myself another hairdresser. I hope this will not happen yet awhile. This was not a kind thought, but I realised all too clearly that one day Lisa too will start developing wrinkles and a double chin, just like everyone else. I disliked myself intensely for thinking this, but it meant nothing, because I often dislike myself. I've been aware for a long while now that I am not really a very nice person, and I've grown used to it. My best trait is that I'm not oppressive, and leave people in peace, but even this stems from a deep feeling of inadequacy. Avoiding things that are frightening or ugly doesn't help at all. Ugliness and terror catch us all up in the end. You can't run away from them for ever. At some point they corner you; and when they do, you may well wish yourself blind and deaf and numb, but the wish is not always granted.

Lisa settled me under the dryer and gave me a couple of magazines to leaf through. I didn't feel like reading, so I closed my eyes. These days I read less and less. Sometimes I feel that reading was only invented to draw people's attention away from things that are really important. What these things might be, though, I have no idea, and with my talent for speculation I probably never shall. Thinking gets you nowhere, it is merely a habit. Occasionally, when I manage not to think, I see pictures, and I reckon that is more helpful for me – even when I can't interpret the pictures.

As the warm air blew round my head I saw, behind my closed lids, one of these pictures. A monstrous creation made of greyish brown paper, like the chrysalis of an insect, hanging from a silvery thread. It looked dead, but at the same time not dead, seeing that underneath the crinkly skin there appeared to be movements going on – little wave-like pulsings and beatings, struggling and urgent. Something inside was trying to emerge.

Then the skin split apart in one spot and I caught a glimpse of a metallic blue shine, and I forced my eyes open wide. I didn't want to see the creature – whatever it was – come out. It was too early still, it must wait inside its casing. I could accustom myself to the grey-brown chrysalis, but the new creature might take me by surprise, and I didn't want to be surprised.

As a child I remember how frightened I used to be of having surprises sprung on me. I used to think they would make me fall down dead. I was too young to know exactly what it meant, to be dead, but I imagined that after the surprise I wouldn't be able to exist any more. This fear has never really left me; I have merely learnt to live with it. And nowadays the idea of not being able to exist any more no longer seems so bad.

I deliberately kept my eyes wide open. I couldn't see Lisa anywhere: her face would have been a tonic. So instead I tried to distract myself by planning a big window-clean in the coming days. In the sunlight the panes already looked smeared and opaque. After window-cleaning I can usually sleep very well. Because the sad fact of it is that I, who was once a champion sleeper, now only sleep out of habit. Sleep is no longer a panacea, it is just a lame escape.

My heated face in the mirror looked flushed and young. Later on this artificial bloom would fade. Without the rollers to tauten the skin, my cheeks would fall a bit, and the skin would droop loosely over my flesh. But who cared: the main thing about being young is not the taut skin but the hope. Each new day you wake up with the hope of experiencing something new; any day, any moment, that big something is going to happen – you have no idea what it will be, but you know it's going to come. I don't remember when this hope died in me, but at least there is still one thing for me to cling to: namely, the hope that one day I will draw a bird that is not completely alone in the world. This will show clearly by the way it holds it head, or the way its little claws are placed, or simply by the colour of its feathers. This bird is asleep somewhere inside me, and all I have to do is wake it up. It is a task I must accomplish on my own. But then what will happen, I ask myself? After this hour of triumph, what? Which is perhaps the reason I never get around to drawing this bird: because I realise it would make no difference to anyone in the world if I did, not even to myself. The hope is unconnected to me; it simply uses me as the means to an end. But what end?

A shadow flitted across the mirror and vanished. And how do things stand with Hubert, I wonder? Was does he hope for? For a long while he dreamed of building a house, and then he inherited one. It wasn't his house at all, but it put paid to his dream. Sometimes I'm afraid Hubert has no hopes any more. I can't be sure of this, though, because we neither of us ever speak about such matters.

Lisa came and turned the dryer down a notch, and I suddenly noticed how unpleasantly hot it had been. How come she was aware of this before I was? Wonderful Lisa, who always knows exactly the right thing to do. What does she daydream about while she is setting people's hair? About new curtains for her bedroom, or a rosy future for her little daughter who is so unlike her? I know what the little girl dreams of: she dreams of being lovingly tucked up in bed at night by her mother. I bet she is allowed to slip into Lisa's bed now and then to warm her toes. It comforts me to know that such lucky little girls exist. My mother was not a good mother. I came into the world by chance – upsetting the rhythms of a household where the only important thing was the curve of my father's fever chart. I am not a good mother either, I am not even a good wife. I do my best, but it's of no service to anyone.

I couldn't turn my head under the dryer: I saw Lisa disappear, but only out of the corner of my eye. A flash of pale mauve, and she was gone. Wearily I closed my eyes again. The chrysalis was still there. It no longer hung from a silver thread, but lay on a table. Anxiously I watched the twitching and pulsing beneath the grey skin. The unborn creature's movements were becoming heftier: any minute now the brittle outer casing would burst asunder. I opened my eyes quickly but it was too late: a purplish red eye had spotted me. It was an evil-looking eye, and I tried hard to forget this creature, nesting there behind my lids.

Then came a click, and the soft hum of air around my head turned to silence. Lisa came and lifted the dryer, and somehow managed to tame my rebellious hair and comb it into shape. I said something about the south wind, and Lisa told me that her mother could forecast it thirty-six hours before it started blowing. I was very surprised to hear that Lisa had a mother. Then she held up a mirror to show me the back of my head, and there was nothing left for me to do but to stand up, pay my bill, and leave this fragrant feminine room, with its mauve and silver décor, and the welcome sight of Lisa's face. I slipped a tip into her overall pocket, and she thanked me – neither humbly nor haughtily but in the completely natural way of one person thanking another for a small gift. Her dark eyes shone warmly behind the long curve of her lids. I was tempted to touch her milky-coffee coloured cheek but refrained. In fact I deliberately hurried out of the door without a backward glance. It would be nice to take Lisa home and keep her under a glass case, but it wouldn't be much fun for her.

Outside it was really warm, and I could feel my ears burning, the way they always do when I've been under the dryer. This is bad enough in winter when it freezes; in muggy weather it's even worse. Not that anyone would notice. Who gives a fig for my ears and what they look like? Besides, everyone seemed to be in such a rush – the lunch-break must have already started. The only exception was a group of pupils from a nearby school, who sauntered along, chattering to one another in what was, to me, a totally foreign language. I imagine Ilse speaks this language to her school friends too, although she never uses it with me. In this respect nothing has changed since my own day: all young people live in two different worlds and are so relaxed about it that they slip easily from one world to the other. I feel very close to young people still – it is just that I seem to have ventured a little farther ahead than they have, into a world that is crueller and colder and more despairing. Very soon these same children will move forward too, never again to return to this muggy February day. Human beings don't revolve in an orbit, they journey from a glowing centre-point outwards, first into a rosy warmth, then into a blue chill, and later into a grey twilight, before their final extinction in the blackness of the night.

I didn't really think this through; I merely saw, very clearly, a swarm of shooting stars, torn from the radius of the hot mother-star, slowly fizzling out in the gelid reaches of space. It didn't mean anything. These things happen all the time; we can only register their occurrence. There is no reason behind them, no intention to help or to hinder. It's is a good thing to remember this fact, although why I should find it consoling, I have no idea.

The warm wind caressed my face, as much as to say, don't worry, that's the way it is. I saw myself, as a child, running through a park. I was crying, and other children were running after me, calling me names. I was afraid and angry and tears were running down into my mouth. The wind dried my tears, leaving a prickly feeling, perhaps on account of the salt. The children stopped shouting, the way they always did, and instead of being mean and cruel they were suddenly my best friends. They held hands with me and together we ran face on into the wind. At times they were my enemies and at times my friends – I never knew why this was, and neither did they.

I had broken into a run myself now, and as I entered the little corner café I was slightly out of breath. I wanted to have a snack before going on to visit Serafine in hospital. It is odd that Madam Magistrate never cooked for herself but left all the work to Serafine, who acted as cook and housemaid and nanny to her, and in the end as nurse. Serafine is eighty now, and at last she too can afford to be ill. There was nothing very special about her, ever. You couldn't even like her, she was so characterless. Hubert never mentions her, and yet she used to feed him and cart him around with her and, later on, clean his shoes for him and iron his shirts. At the end of each month a standing allowance is paid into her bank account: her small pension would not even cover the cost of a single room in the rest home. If I bring up her name, Hubert gets cross. He never visits her either, and I'm sorry about this, although I confess that I do so only very reluctantly myself. When she sees me approaching I can read the disappointment in her face. She never learns: she is disappointed afresh, each time. I only hope that Ferdinand's visits cheer her up a bit more than mine do. Secretly, I think, she resents me coming, although she never actually throws my gifts back in my face. There was never much sympathy between us, mainly because she knew I was an obstacle in Madam Magistrate's path. I suggested once to Hubert that we have her to live with us in the house, but he turned the idea down. She reminds him of the past, and he doesn't want to be reminded – I understand that very well. But this hard streak in him, that only rarely comes to the fore, frightens me. He has quite simply pushed Serafine out of his mind: he was always very rational when it came to doing that. Serafine is quite contented in the rest home, and Hubert pays the fees generously so that she has a little bit of spending money as well. His rationality is awesome – so cold and hard that it reminds me of his mother's. But one sees it so seldom that I tend to forget about it. The elder Ferdinand would never have put Serafine in a rest home, and would have caused us a great deal of upset on this account. But then he was not so rational.

I sat down at a little marble table, and my thoughts ran through the corridors of an underground labyrinth – an ant hill with no plan to it at all. Underground paths have always frightened me. During the bombing raids I'd much rather have taken refuge in the park than in the cellar. Now I was well and truly lost, and it was only thanks to the waiter that I found my way back to the surface. He bent over my table to take my order. I asked for zabaglione and a cup of tea.

This café is pleasantly old fashioned, with faded red plush seats and fringed silk curtains – a real museum setting. The tables are widely spaced, so you don't get anyone eavesdropping on your conversation or reading your newspaper over your shoulder. You sit on a private island where all that's to be heard is the tinkle of spoons and the rustling of pages. I come here whenever I have things to do in town. The clientele consists mainly of elderly people, plus a few office girls who come in for their lunch break, and the odd chance customer now and again; how the proprietor makes his living from such scant trade is a mystery. In the back somewhere there's a room when young people come to play billiards, but you hardly hear them at all.

Sitting at the next table to mine was a young woman – or an oldish girl – writing a letter. It's ages since I wrote a proper letter myself. Hardly surprising when you consider that I broke off all my past friendships, which were never real friendships anyway. Before this strange illness of mine, which kept me out of the social swim for two whole years, I knew a lot of people who appeared to share my interests, but those two years were enough to sever all the ties that bound us. Occasionally I meet someone from that period by chance on the street, and we greet each other politely and exchange a few words, and that is it. I probably miss a lot, due to my reserve, but it doesn't bother me in the slightest.

The waiter brought the tea and zabaglione and silently withdrew. I have known him for a long time now, and I notice that he is getting increasingly older and slower. One day he won't be here any more, and for a short while I will miss him. The egg of the zabaglione tasted stale, the way eggs always do nowadays. I don't wonder: they no longer come from cheerful free-range hens, or so I'm told, but from miserable creatures imprisoned in cages. These eggs are their revenge. I am definitely on the side of the poor prisoners. Their eggs ought to taste even worse, in order to punish us for our crimes. I chased the zabaglione down with a gulp of tea, which didn't taste much like tea either, but at least it took away the eggy taste. Then I wiped my mouth and took a look in my hand mirror: all in order, my ears had gone back to their normal colour and this cheered me up a little.

I have tried everything on the menu in this place, but the only really decent thing is their coffee. Which actually is delicious. Their ham tastes of very salty paper, their fried bacon is rancid, and the sausages are best forgotten. Russian salad is another of their specialities, but nobody ever orders it a second time – the only eatable part is the salad leaves, which taste of grass. In other places things are not much better, merely more expensive, and here you can at least sit in peace and comfort. Hubert says I'm fussy, but I'm not: unfortunately for me I just remember the way food ought to taste.

There were a couple of elderly ladies stuffing themselves with cakes, and I avoided looking at them. I picked up some newspapers instead and started to read. After I had read three totally different versions of the same news item – a burglary, I think it was – with three different renderings of the burglar's name, I gave up. To solve riddles is not what I read the paper for.

Meanwhile a man had entered the café and had sat down facing me, in the middle of the room. I could tell straight away that he was one of the chance customers. A self-confident man, though, seeing that he had chosen a centre table – something I never manage to do myself. He ordered coffee in a voice that reminded me of something but I wasn't sure what. He must have been around fifty: thick salt-and-pepper hair cut very short, corpulent body, slightly droopy cheeks, and a peculiar roll of fat that protruded over the collar of his jacket. I couldn't place him, it was really annoying. Then he turned, and I saw his profile and I recognised him at last. It was old Dr Hofstätter from Rautersdorf, who had attended me when I was a child. I stared at him and was about to go over and greet him when I remembered that Dr Hofstätter must be about eighty by now. That really threw me. If it wasn't the Doctor then it must be his son – the young man I used to go hedgehog hunting with. In those days he was a nice looking boy, lanky and athletic. Where had all these lumps of lard come from? Presumably he had taken over his father's practise and was now a busy GP; it was plain to see that he lived in the county. If the war hadn't come and my grandfather hadn't died, I could even have married this man and gone on living peacefully in Rautersdorf to this day.

It was hard to imagine. I suddenly felt pleased that I wasn't living in Rautersdorf, married to this man, raising all his children – for there were bound to have been four or five. I would not have fallen ill, or if I had, it wouldn't have been so bad. This man would never have sent me away: he was strong enough to have gone on living with a deaf wife. He would have taken good care of me, and betrayed me diligently, the way a normal man would in such circumstances.

I waited for some emotion to arise in me but felt nothing; a part of me sat by and mocked the attempts of the other part to revivify the past. I could clearly remember those summer nights, the smell of hay and the rustlings of the hedgehogs, but the memories had nothing to do with the stranger sitting there at the centre table. I had even forgotten his Christian name. He had the appearance of a kind family doctor and at the same time of a man who rides roughshod over everyone, but then that is a very frequent mixture.

I called for the waiter, paid my bill, put on my coat and left. As I passed in front of the café window the man raised his head and looked me straight in the eye. He frowned, perplexed, and appeared to be thinking hard – even when hedgehog hunting he had been slower on the uptake than I was. I took refuge in a nearby doorway and waited. Three minutes later he came out again and scanned the street. Then he shook his head and went back into the café. He had recognised me too, but that wasn't so difficult, I had changed far less than he had. Outwardly, I mean. I slipped out of the doorway and continued on my way, light hearted, like one who has escaped from danger. Rautersdorf was dead and must stay dead. The Rautersdorf inside my head is my own creation, a huge picture that I have painted myself and that admits of no alteration. In this picture my grandfather walks through the clearings where the wood lies stacked, and hunters come home through the mist at close of day. A cow is led to the bull; children splash around in puddles; unripe walnuts hang on the trees, and my grandfather puts walnut leaves in his footbath because they are so soothing to the feet. The banks of the Danube are white with snowdrops, sun beats down on the golden corn-fields, honey drips from green hives, and a loaf of bread lies on the table. Grasshoppers chirp during the long summer nights, and the frogs croak, and every so often an apple falls onto the wet grass.

This is the way things will always remain in my picture. It is out of my hands now; I have no more power to change things. Of course there is an element of magic in it, but I have always been quite proficient in magic. Nowadays I use it only in tiny doses, and sometimes I think I've lost the knack altogether, but magic is like swimming and riding a bicycle – you never really forget. I use it for Hubert's sake mainly. I hope he dies before I do, because I don't know how he would manage without these little spells that I manage to work. Ferdinand has inherited my talent, but I'm not at all sure that he uses it in a noble fashion: sometimes he shows the makings of a real warlock. The thought of Ferdinand made me smile, and in my mind I hugged him tight to me, wherever he might be, and let him go again. Immediately I saw him make off fast in a different direction, but that was as it should be: warlocks must walk a solitary path.

I decided I was quite mad. The wind blew into my hair, fluffing out Lisa's artistic styling. 'I love you, wind,' I told it, and a woman looked at me sharply. I laughed right into her face and left her staring after me, nonplussed. I enjoy walking through the streets of this city, I like covering long distances on foot.

Then I suddenly remembered Serafine, and the enchantment vanished. Up till now the day had been so nice, I had felt light hearted and tireless and young. All gone now. My pace slowed and I switched to feeling very old. It's strange, I always feel either old or young but never my right age. My shoulders sagged, and I dragged my feet like a tired old crone.

Serafine was in a public ward with eight beds to it. It looked as if all the old or dying patients had been clumped here together so as not to disturb the others. That they might disturb one another was evidently of no account. In the beds lay wizened little midget ladies and bloated giantesses, all desperately ill. I have a weakness for old people and I am patient with them, especially when they aren't up and moving but are lying, docile, in their beds. Nevertheless, I don't like coming here. Several of these old women will die where they are; the others will be put on their feet and sent home again, where their relatives are probably dreading their return.

The air in this room is unpleasant, but it is not that which repels me: it is the will to life which I sense like a dense, enveloping cloud, pressing on me from all sides. These poor creatures give off, not only the odour of sick bodies, but the smell of the fierce tenacity with which they cling to life. A few of them will have given up – those on the verge of death, maybe – but the remainder go on hoping against hope.

I come to see Serafine every ten days or so. She's already been here seven weeks, and this was my fifth visit. Her bed is by the window; as I pass I greet the occupants of the other beds on both sides of the ward. Some of them recognise me, but I never remember which. Ten days ago Serafine was slightly better, and it looked as if she might pull through. The fact is, she stopped living when Madam Magistrate died. She was lost without someone to give her orders. Her relatives, wherever they were from, all died long ago, and her mistress was everything to her: mother, employer, sister, and finally child.

The lady in the next bed to hers – one of the swollen giantesses – whispered to me: 'We're going downhill, mum. Won't be long now.'

Serafine was not looking out of the window today, but lay staring at the blanket. That was a bad sign: up till now she had always monitored the comings and goings of the orderlies in the courtyard below. 'Here I am, back again, Fini,' I said. 'I've brought you something nice.'

She looked at me, however, as if she wasn't seeing me at all. I placed my hand on her thin, freckled arm, but still she didn't move. 'Fini,' I said, 'I'm Hubert's wife. Do you recognise me?'

'Hubert', she repeated flatly, and began to mumble something. She mumbled very fast and I couldn't understand a word. She had not put her dentures in today, either. 'Is that you, Anna?' she suddenly asked very clearly, and her small heart-shaped face took on an unhealthy flush. 'Where am I, and who is going to milk the cow?'

Very slowly and clearly I explained to her what had happened and assured her she was getting better. It was a lie, of course, but what can you say on these occasions?

It didn't seem to interest her at all. She went on asking after her mother, wanted to know whether she was still ill, and who was taking care of the livestock. She called me a slut, told me I was letting everything go to pieces, said I couldn't even be trusted to look after a cow – I think she mistook me for one of her dead sisters. I was filled with sadness: some terrible change had taken place in Serafine.

The woman in the next bed heaved herself up, stuck out a blue-coloured leg from under the blankets, and said: 'This has been going on for five days now; she doesn't recognise anyone, and at nights she gets so restless.'

So then I started telling Serafine that her mother was feeling better now, and that I was taking good care of the cow, and that she needn't trouble herself about anything. 'A chunk of wood fell on your head,' I explained to her, 'but you're going to get well again soon. The cow is in really good fettle.'

I went on so long, and in such detail, that in the end I had almost persuaded myself I was indeed the slutty Anna, with a sick mother to look after and a cow to milk. Then I peeled an orange for Serafine, who was gradually calming down a little, and she grabbed it from my hand and sucked at it greedily. This provoked a coughing fit, and the orange juice ran down her chin and onto her neck. I dried it with a handkerchief. No sooner was the fit over than she reached out to the bedside table for the remaining slices of orange and crammed them into her mouth: from the speed at which she swallowed them, she could have been dying of hunger. After that she collapsed back on the pillow and lay there motionless, her fingers plucking at the blanket. She seemed to have forgotten all about me.

This plucking movement was a sign that the end was near, her neighbour told me knowingly: she had often observed it to be so. She spoke loudly, as if Serafine couldn't hear us or was already as good as dead, and this annoyed me. I made no reply.

All of a sudden Serafine looked at me and said, 'You're a cunning one, eh. So he married you in the end, that two-timer?'

'Yes,' I said, 'in the end he more or less had to.'

She let out a chuckle. She was expressing herself, I noticed, in a way that Madam Magistrate would never have sanctioned. But then there was no Madam Magistrate in her life any more, so what need was there to act ladylike and refined? After this she went back to staring at the blanket and picking at it with her fingers. The neighbouring lady, a ring of satisfaction in her voice, made another comment on the meaning of this unmistakable sign.

I went on sitting by Serafine's bed for another quarter of an hour, but it felt like a long time. She looked very young today. Once upon a time she must have been a sweet and pretty young girl, but ever since I'd known her myself her little heart-shaped face had been stamped by weakness and stupidity. A good, stupid, dutiful nonentity that went by the name of Serafine; a person to whom life had always come second-hand. But what did I know about her life, really? Nothing, save the fact that she was my mother-in-law's slave.

When I stood up to leave she turned towards me, and I knew that she had finally recognised me. Her gaze was totally steady and lucid, and at the same time she looked much older than before. She blinked at me and said, 'I'm done for.' The expression seemed to please her because she repeated it twice: 'Done for.

take on a silvery sheen, which may have something to do with the lighting in the room. Being unable to hear him, I naturally concentrate on his outward appearance, and what strikes me most forcibly is the eyes, set so far apart that they hardly seem human. Sometimes, when his face reaches brick-red its colour suddenly fades and turns almost green. I observe all this, and with the opening and closing of the mouth I observe his teeth too, which are fairly regular, and his tongue and gums. Which means he must be shouting, because you don't normally get to see people's gums when they talk. And all the time while he is talking (or whispering or shouting) his hands are living quite a separate life. They are big, white, stubby hands, overgrown with bright red hairs. I watch them a lot, in preference to the face, which disgusts me. They clamp into fists, bang on the table; I can feel the vibrations through my entire body. Then they open again and lie there, flat, tired and spent. A short while later they crawl towards one another and start up a writhing movement: one hand tries to throttle the other or to tear off a finger. At times the struggle is so intense that you can see drops of blood on the skin. X appears not to notice. His fingernails are pointed, unsuited to such broad hands, and are stained with nicotine. While he is talking he forgets to smoke, but the room reeks of stale smoke all the same. I never smoke when I'm there. I reckon it's best to sit there calmly, watching his mad act; if I smoked, it might work on him as a stimulant. Those animals that are his hands could easily opt to strangle me rather than each other. But they do not dare: their master has ordered them not to touch me; for the moment I am a precious commodity that he cannot afford to lose.

So there I sit and watch. His silent shouting wears me down. I have always hated hearing shouts: to have to watch them is nigh unbearable. But strangely I no longer have the wish to avert my gaze the way I did to start with: on the contrary, it seems important not to lose sight of the hands, even though they have begun to disturb me even more than the face. They are so naked and explicit, and so utterly devoid of shame.

Why I keep going there, I honestly don't know. It could be because

135

it draws me back into a world I had almost forgotten. Or it could be because it is better to be in the company of a horrible human being than of no human being at all, and because the atmosphere in his room reminds me of what humans smell of: namely, sweat, fear, hatred and stale smoke. 'Are you completely on your own?' X wrote on his note pad, and I replied, 'Yes, completely.' That seemed to reassure him. It is the truth, I am totally on my own and on the point of becoming like my magpie – not like a real magpie but like the one in my drawing: cold, mean and cut off from the world entirely. When X pours me out coffee his maltreated hands tremble, and his face is white and sunken. To my surprise I feel almost sorry for him because I realise that he needs me far more than I need him.

Soon I may be able to go to the village to do my own shopping. For a few days now I've been sleeping better. It is as if X, with his ghastly confessions, were drawing all the energy out of me and making me empty and relaxed, ready for a full night's sleep.

In its way, the magpie drawing has come out rather well: it makes me freezing cold just to look at it. Tomorrow I will lock it away in the cupboard, out of sight, and the day after I will go to the village. This time I ought to manage it all right.

November 26th

A new commission: fish and other sea creatures for a children's book. The book is pretty daft: all the fish and starfish and crabs and so forth bursting with friendliness and noble sentiments. My drawings won't fit the bill at all, but I doubt anyone will notice. To have to illustrate a book like this fills me with malicious glee.

Hubert writes that he has found a place for us to live – a three roomed apartment that needs doing up and furnishing. This will take a while, he says, because the building is an old one, and for the moment he has run out of money, but when all is ready we will be together again. Poor Hubert, what will he do when the apartment is furnished? His letters always contain a veiled reproach: Look, I'm doing everything I can to mend things between us, don't you think it's time you did something too and put an end to this dreary deafness lark? I wrote back telling him that for the time being he need send me no more money.

While I'm out – and I'm out every day now, despite the bad weather – someone comes into my room and snoops around. As far as I can tell they touch nothing apart from my drawings, which are always arranged differently from the way in which I left them. My diary notes are hidden under the mattress: if someone were to disturb those I would notice straight away. But the snooper, whoever it is, seems to be interested only in my pictures and the contents of the drawer in my writing table. I keep nothing there but my correspondence with publishers: Hubert's letters I burn straight away. So my visitor is not very intelligent. The gamekeeper has never shown any interest in my belongings, therefore I think it must be his lady friend who is the guilty party. Either way, I couldn't care less. The gamekeeper eyes me disapprovingly; he always has done, but now there is a new look on his face, a knowing look, a despising look, very much man to woman: he has followed me and knows where I go. Presumably he thinks X is my lover.

For the first time it seems to have dawned on him that I am not a sexless being, and the result is not very pleasant. Perhaps he is wondering if he ought to inform Hubert of what is going on, hesitating between his duty as caretaker and his fear – should Hubert then come and fetch me – of forfeiting his pay. Or perhaps, more likely still, he wants to blackmail me and doesn't quite know how to go about it. Anyway, I told X in future not to shout so loud: I couldn't hear him myself, but anyone prowling round in the vicinity could. He turned ashen with fear, and since then he does his utmost to speak more quietly, showing far less tongue and gums. The strain, however, tells on his hands: they behave ever more murderously to one another and are now covered in blue bruises. Sometimes they reach up towards the neck as if to strangle him, or start tearing at his hair. I am beginning to pity him: whatever he has done, he is paying for it dearly.

I can't really work out what he's doing here: he's clearly not a country person, doesn't belong here at all. His worktable – an old, rickety piece of furniture – is covered with newspapers. No books to be seen, just newspapers – every single paper he can obtain in the village. Maybe he walks through the woods like I do, or maybe he just sits in his room reading the papers over and over and waiting for me. Sometimes he behaves in a humble way, almost servile, and I can tell that he is unaccustomed to behaving like that. It is only fear that prompts him: he wants to make a good impression on me in order not to lose me.

When I leave he watches me with hungry eyes, like a big ugly dog that is afraid his master will not be coming back. I imagine him throwing himself down on the bed afterwards and falling asleep, exhausted. It's possible that he can only sleep after I have been to see him. He's not looking well, he's lost weight and his skin seems to have grown too loose for him. I place him around forty, I doubt he is any older than that; he's just in bad shape. There are times, when he is speaking, that it's a wonder he doesn't drop dead on the floor: his voice is controlled through sheer will power and he turns purple in the face. There are other times when his eyes blaze, not with hatred, but with a wild joy. They turn black and cloudy, and then I feel afraid. At such moments his hands are relaxed and contented like two sated beasts thinking back on a rich meal.

All this is bearable, but he should never let himself laugh: one of these days he'll break his neck. He throws his head right back, and I can see the sweat on his neck and the bright red of his gums. He laughs and laughs until the stool nearly tips over. I sit there calmly with that look on my face that reassures him I can't hear a word. So then he bends forward and talks to me confidentially, glancing anxiously to right and left out of the corners of his eyes, and I know that he is telling me the worst things of all. His face comes so close that I can smell his breath: he must smoke like a chimney. I have a feeling he used to drink a lot and regrets he no longer can: who knows, under the influence of alcohol he might start talking to someone who is not deaf. By the time I leave, his shirt is drenched in sweat and clinging fast to his body.

I wander back, half numb inside, and my room seems to me like a corner of heaven – a clean-smelling, peaceful corner of heaven. My pictures greet me, and I know I have come home. I owe this knowledge to X and am grateful. I curl up in my leather chair, watch the twilight seep into the room, and feel very tired. Something is happening inside me, something new. I don't know what will come of it. In the end everything is a mystery and I resign myself to the fact. It is a nice feeling to give up struggling and resign yourself.

January 1st

At my request Hubert didn't come here for Christmas. It was my Christmas present to him. He writes that little Ferdinand was thrilled by the Christmas tree. The apartment is still not ready; the window fittings are being painted and he has caught a cold from the draught. It would have been better to wait and have them painted in the spring, but he's already paying rent for the place and wants to move in as soon as possible. He is working hard for our future. I take this to mean that Hubert is very busy and that for him time passes quickly. My time passes at a different pace, but he is not to know this, it doesn't emerge from my letters. I write seldom, and when I do I use dutiful, schoolgirl phases: 'I agree with you entirely' and 'I am feeling a lot better'.

The more I see of X the closer I feel drawn to Hubert. It makes me realise how far I had drifted away from him. I think of the words human beings use to one another, and I remember Hubert's tenderness during our nights together. And I remember how we used to laugh. I am too corrupted now for all that; even if I should hear again it would never be the same as before. Separating us lie whole tracts of experience that I have been through alone and about which I could never tell him. But I must give him a chance, and for that reason I am going to ask for a divorce. It's not too late for him yet; he may possibly have another woman in his life already. What place do I have in Hubert's orderly existence – I who sit with X every day and receive his outpourings of filth and hatred? But then, what do I know about Hubert's existence? Only a part; the rest he keeps to himself.

Sometimes I am afraid that the hours I spend with X will change me in some way that I cannot foresee. Almost certainly he is a monster now, but what used he to be? A person can be changed into a monster without realising it. One part of them is transformed, while the other part crouches, shivering, in its dark hideout, going slowly mad with anguish. X's hands have gone mad already, there is no telling what they may get up to. He doesn't even know this himself. It is already something that the poor, trapped creature inside him can get out for a couple of hours and scream its misery to the world. The world being me – a deaf woman who sits there with an attentive expression on her face as if she is listening.

For two weeks now I have been doing my own shopping. Progress, but towards what? It's easy, I just pass my note across the counter and the shop lady fills up my basket. I'm so far away in my thoughts that I hardly notice people's pity or curiosity.

I've stopped bothering about myself. Even if a raven should stare at me with curiosity I wouldn't care. Although ravens wouldn't do that, of course, because they are decent, well behaved birds; all they would do is turn their heads away and look into the distance.

When I came up from the cellar, having consigned this last batch of notes to the flames, Hubert was still sitting at his desk. He had sought consolation in a book about the battle of Ebelsberg. 'It's extremely interesting, this,' he said. 'I don't think I'll bother with television this evening, but you go ahead if you like.'

'If all the same to you,' I said, 'I think I'll go back upstairs and draw a bit.'

'Fine,' said Hubert. 'You do whatever you like.'

I didn't really want to go back up to the loft: it is no longer the same since I've been forced to read my old diary entries there. But there was nowhere else to go. It can't go on much longer, anyway; these packets will soon stop. I can't remember how much I wrote, but not much more, surely. Then I will air the room out and do my best to forget this week.

I sat down at my table and half-heartedly set about drawing a nuthatch. I drew for ten minutes at a time, getting up in the intervals and walking around a bit. But while I was walking I was unable to see the nuthatch clearly in my mind's eye. The drawing started taking on reptilian characteristics, and that I did not like. It is true that nuthatches have a rather flat shape, but this one, with every line I added, was looking more and more like a lizard. In the end it turned into a hybrid, and I had the feeling that I didn't really want to draw either a nuthatch or a lizard but something quite different that I couldn't visualise. It was very annoying, and after a couple of hours I tore the strange creature up and threw it in the waste paper basket. I don't often do that: unsuccessful drawings are important too. This, however, was not an unsuccessful drawing, it was an un*wished* drawing. Maybe I would never be able to draw again. This thought worried me so much that before going to bed I had to take a sleeping pill, and even then I lay there for a long time, dozing and feeling befuddled but not really sleeping.

Beside me, Hubert breathed peacefully and regularly: the battle of Ebelsberg had taken due effect.

Friday

In the afternoon, when Hubert had had his nap and left, I lay on the sofa in the living room and tried to read the paper. The sofa was still warm from Hubert's body, and I was very tired, having slept little during the night. The weather was overcast and the room was rather dark. It is an impossible task, to read a newspaper lying down. After tussling with it a bit and failing to turn the pages I let it drop on the floor and turned my face to the wall. I realised I was no longer young, or not young enough, at any rate, to be able to deal with a thick yellow envelope arriving every day.

I didn't want to think about this though. Today's package lay in the loft, and I felt proud of having had the discipline not to open it straight away, read its contents and burn it. These letters have nothing to do with my life as a housewife and I'm not going to let them upset my daily routine. I do as a matter of fact manage to forget them for hours on end, but *only* for hours, not longer. When I have burnt the lot I will reflect carefully on the whole business. Not that it will get me anywhere, reflecting never does, it's just a habit I have since kindergarten. I must have been taught it by my grandfather; that is why it is so ingrained in me. No doubt he meant well – after all, how was he to know that my head wasn't geared to thinking? And in the end he must have discovered for himself how little it had helped him personally – all that analysing and dissecting. His brain was so clear and tidy: he had planned his entire life and that of his children and grandchildren, but without taking into account that other people's heads were not so orderly. Hence the shipwreck of his plans.

But anyway, I still follow his counsel like a robot, and go on thinking when, for me, there is no point in it at all.

I was so tired that I was shivering. I knew I must either go and get a blanket or else put up with the discomfort, but before I could decide which course to follow I fell fast asleep. I had a dream. I dreamed I was looking down on an unfamiliar landscape, hovering in the air above it and moving around with little flapping motions of my hands. I was the first human being who could fly; I had just discovered how to. It was the easiest thing in the world, all I had to do was abandon myself to the air currents like a swimmer does to water. Beneath me glittered a dark blue expanse of water, ruffled by tiny waves, and beyond it rose the bright green slope of a mountain. For a moment I was afraid, but the fear passed. I knew I couldn't fall: a flap of the hands was enough to carry me right over water and mountain. The air was cool, pleasantly so. The sky was dark blue like the water, and vault-shaped, decked with little clouds. There were no houses in sight, nor people nor animals. Very slowly I did a somersault, then gave a couple of flaps and glided on my way, holding my head high and feeling the cool air brush my cheeks. The countryside soon disappeared and I found myself passing over a city – an ugly, abandoned city, dotted with ruins. In the middle of a small square some people were standing, and they looked up at me, angry and mistrustful: to them I was evidently something alien – and an enemy alien, even though I was doing nothing worse than float around in the air. Then I remembered that human beings were not allowed to fly. These people were observing this rule, but I had forgotten it and I would never abide by it again. All around me were wires and pylons; I beat the air hard, trying to rise above them. This was a mistake, I should have been more cautious: something had caught onto me and was pulling me down. It was hard to resist the pull; I was no longer floating but flapping clumsily like a bat. A few of the people tried to catch at my feet and trap me. I knew they would kill me if they got me because I had broken the rule, but I didn't seem to mind: if I couldn't fly any more, then life was not worth living. I let my arms drop and waited for the end, but as I did so a current of air suddenly lifted me high into the sky again: I had escaped my catchers. Then the city was gone and I was drifting instead over flat grassland. The air was chill now, but I didn't feel the cold because my body temperature too had cooled. The plain was vast and I knew it would go on for ever. There was not even a tree for me to land in, but perhaps I would be able to sleep in the air. Yes, certainly I could. I was floating along on my back now, my hands crossed over my chest, staring up at the sky. Night had fallen and I began to freeze. Stars were all around me, and there was a big white moon. Full of trust, I closed my eyes and went to sleep.

I was woken by the bang of a faulty exhaust pipe in the street outside. It made me furious, and I would have willingly leaned out of the window with a gun in my hand and shot the culprit on the spot. As always when I am woken by a sudden noise, my heart started to behave strangely: it fluttered and gurgled, and it was some time before it resumed its regular beat. My heart hates noise and refuses to get used to it: one day a shock will stop it dead. I thought back on the time when I lived in total silence: perhaps it had been a defence mechanism and I hadn't realised it. A vague nostalgia rose in me for those far off years, but I found this so unacceptable that I refused to believe it. I retrieved the newspaper from the floor and set about folding it tidily for Hubert's sake, then I placed it on his desk. Untidiness really upsets him, and on no account do I want him upset.

It was three o'clock. The dream was still fresh in my mind. Why couldn't I fly, I wondered? I stood on the carpet and flapped my hands but nothing happened. How could it, when I had no faith in what I was doing? My body weighed on me like an unbearable burden, heavy as stone. A stone can never fly. It seemed as if my feet were about to break through the floor, dragging me down to the cellar and then deeper still into the centre of the earth where this body belonged. Wearily I picked up my feet and began to stagger across the floor like a colossus. It was so sad but at the same time so funny that I couldn't help laughing: it was ridiculous to behave like this at my age. Then I suddenly realised that it wasn't ridiculous at all, and that nothing

I did was ridiculous if I felt like doing it. Ridiculous was just a word that had lost all meaning for me, a word I had erased from my vocabulary. It was nice to know I need no longer fear the judgement of others. I had minded so much in my youth about what other people thought of me, but now at long last this fear had gone. Or maybe it had been gone for some time and I had only just now noticed it: I am often slow to realise what is going on inside me.

As I set about laying the tea table for the Nice Lady it struck me that what I was doing was quite unnecessary: I was merely doing it out of habit. There was no need for me even to open the door to her; I could easily say, 'Go back home, I'm not in the right mood to see you today,' or, 'Do you mind if we have pickled onions instead of tea and cakes? It's so much less trouble.' I imagined the face she would make, and started to laugh again, but meanwhile I went on making all the right preparations: boiled the kettle, made the tea, and put the cake on a serving plate. The Nice Lady was always punctual, you could count on her to arrive on time.

I went to the bathroom to tidy myself up a bit, and in the mirror I noticed that the pillow had left two deep imprints on my cheek, from temple to ear lobe. Nothing I could do about them – marks like that take hours to fade. I dabbed on some face powder but only cursorily: why shouldn't I show a stripy face? The triumphant feeling of my dream had not yet vanished entirely. It struck me that I might now understand birds better, and my drawing disaster of the evening before seemed less important. Then the bell rang and I went down to open the door.

In came the Nice Lady. I still haven't a clue whether I like her or not, but I've known her for fifteen years now and every time I see her she astounds me. She is a human being like me, and female like me, and we gave birth to a baby at the same time, but apart from this I can discover nothing that we have in common. Why does she keep coming to see me, I ask myself each time? I am bad company – for Nice Ladies, at any rate, to whom my magic is useless since they cannot understand it. In fact I am only good company for the very old or the very young: adults in between are so different from me that they make me shy, and the Nice Lady is quintessentially an adult. Sometimes when she is sitting there beside me I get the feeling she is going to fall fast asleep and slip under the table from sheer boredom. Nor would I blame her if she did: every sentence I utter bores me stiff too. On the contrary, though, not only does she not slip under the table but she appears to be delighted by our conversation. The Nice Lady remains one of the greatest unsolved mysteries of my life. To me she is a rare specimen of an extinct species; I have tried hard to study her but have never uncovered her secret.

The Nice Lady is nice, of that there is no doubt. She looks nice too – tall, thin and very well groomed. She wears her natural blond hair in a timeless style, her face is on the long side and her expression is pleasant and withdrawn. Her eyes are blue, but not a clear blue, and they are slightly too close set. Her whole head has a narrow look about it, as if someone had pressed it in gently from the sides. I find the eyes a bit off-putting because they are so small and close, but that is only an aesthetic consideration.

The Nice Lady has a husband who is handsome and a good achiever and from the looks of him could be her brother. Their four children take after their parents, study hard at school and behave well, but not unnaturally so. All this I have learnt from conversations and photographs, because I've never set foot in the Nice Lady's house. They don't have a television, and they pass their evenings playing games and reading and making music. The husband is a civil servant, works in a ministry, and finds plenty of quality time for his family: they go on walking tours in the summer and skiing holidays in winter, all specially arranged so that the youngest children can take part in everything too. They never travel abroad, and they spend their summer holidays in the country somewhere, always at the same spot. The children range from fifteen to nine and they all play some instrument. I reckon the Nice Lady is a good ten years younger than I am but she looks ageless and could be anywhere between thirty and fifty. If anyone were to record our conversations they would sound like some huge misunderstanding from beginning to end.

Anyway, in she came, took off her black Persian lamb coat (a pretty but old fashioned garment), and stepped into the sitting room. Underneath the coat she was wearing a costume, medium blue like her eyes, well cut and of very good material. A row of pearls, flat-heeled black shoes and a black handbag completed her toilette. From the handbag she extracted a small leather purse, drew from it a handkerchief and blew her nose. This she performed with inimitable discretion, turning her head away and to one side.

I sat and stared at her. Once she had finished she tucked the handkerchief away again in the purse, popped the purse back into the handbag and clipped it shut with a smile. 'The weather doesn't look like being as fine as it was yesterday, unfortunately,' she said.

'No,' I said. 'It's pretty nasty out.' To use any stronger expression would have been unthinkable in her presence.

'I do so love the springtime,' she confided to me with another smile.

I set before her a couple of magazines – the tidiest I could find in my haste – and fled to the kitchen on the excuse of making coffee. Once there I tried to pull myself together. I told myself sternly that the Nice Lady was just a human being and therefore there was nothing to get worked up about; nevertheless I promised myself to say nothing to provoke her or offend her in any way. Only a monster of discourtesy could do a thing like that, and I didn't want to act like a monster. The only trouble was, I'm never quite sure what offends her and what doesn't. In certain matters she is as prudish as . . . well, as anyone can be nowadays and more so; in others she sometimes says things that shock even me.

At last I got the coffee poured out and the cake sliced, and the conversation proper could begin:

Nice Lady: 'This coffee is simply delicious.'

147

Me: 'Well, at least it's not bitter.'

Nice Lady: 'No, it's not bitter in the least.'

Silence

Nice Lady: 'Have you seen *Dr Zhivago?*'

Me: 'No, we hardly ever go to the cinema.'

Nice Lady: 'It's a masterpiece. You simply must go and see it. It had my husband enthralled.'

Me: 'Isn't it rather long?'

Nice Lady: 'Yes, it is, but one is so captivated one hardly notices the time. And the music . . . !'

Me: 'But the seats in cinemas are so hard.'

Nice Lady, mildly taken aback: 'Surely you don't mean . . . '

Me, quickly: 'No, no, of course not, what I meant . . . '

Nice Lady, gliding tactfully over my faux pas: 'And how is your delightful family getting on?'

This is the moment when I begin to recover my self composure. I tell her we're all fine and begin asking questions about her family. This question grants me about half an hour of respite. Making what I hope are appropriate smiles in the right places, I sit and listen to how her husband is extremely busy at the Ministry but manages to relax in the evenings, playing trains with the children; how little Ewald has had the measles but is now better; how Hildegard, the eldest daughter, is away on a skiing holiday with the school, like Ilse; how Roswitha, the thirteen year old, has had her tonsils out and put on two kilos since the operation; and how Reinhold, aged eleven, tends sometimes to be naughty and to speak before he's spoken to. In punishment he gets no pudding for his supper, says his mother blithely, so things will soon be set back to rights.

I can readily believe it. In that family everything is always soon set back to rights. The Nice Lady likes telling me about her home life, and I sit and duly marvel. To distract myself while she is talking I sometimes imagine terrible things happening instead of those she reports: secret intrigues and wickedness defying description. But then I look into her little mild blue eyes and realise it is impossible. The Nice Lady tells no lies and neither do any members of her family, and if the children are ever led astray, things are explained to them until they understand and repent, and order is swiftly restored.

The Nice Lady is a great one for explanations in every sphere: the papers are full of horrifying stories, are they not, and it's always the fault of the parents for not informing their children properly. While she was pregnant, for example, she was always careful to let the older children become involved: they were allowed to put their ears to her stomach and listen to the heart-beats of the new baby inside. It had filled them with respect for Mother Nature and Her wonderful ways.

When we reach this point I always turn bright red and rush for more coffee. I realise I will never grasp the workings of the Nice Lady's mind: I am too corrupt. Afterwards her conversation turned to other, more distant members of her family circle, to the rising cost of living, and to how Hildegard had touched her so by giving her an album of hand-pressed flowers for Christmas. Her husband, too, had found the gift enchanting.

I can't say I was exactly bored, not yet. I merely sat and listened and tried not to betray my astonishment. The Nice Lady gave two more dainty nose blows – open bag, take out purse, close purse, close bag – and repeated her dismay at the weather being so unseasonable. More like February, alas, but no doubt spring would soon be on its way.

There she sat, a picture in pastel tints, her cheeks rosy, her carriage upright, not a hair out of place, not a vertebra touching the chair-back – I could have swooned from admiration. She seemed to me more enigmatic than any of my birds, and I am already hard put to understand them. I must be a very dull-witted creature. For a long time – just to make their relationship conform better to reality – I used to harbour the thought that the Nice Lady's husband deceived her on the sly, but after once catching sight of him I had to abandon this comforting idea. Not only is he not the deceiving type, but he is not corruptible either, and I doubt he so much as picks his nose – even when he is alone. A glimpse of paradise on earth, and it's my fault if I can't live in such a paradise: I am corrupted through and through. This is especially clear to me after a visit from the Nice Lady and I am especially pleased that it should be so. Why does she keep coming? What does she see in me? It's a mystery I shall never solve.

'This *has* been a nice afternoon,' she said, rising to leave.

'I'm glad you enjoyed it,' I replied. 'I hope we meet up again soon.'

'I hope so too,' she said. 'It's so nice, now and again, to have a real woman-to-woman chat. There are things, aren't there, that you can't really talk about to your husband and children?'

'There are indeed,' I said.

In the hall she paused a moment to powder delicately her rather long nose, then put on her hat and her fur coat and extended a cool, dry hand for me to shake. I was careful not to press it too hard, and suggested that I accompany her to the bus stop. I urgently needed some fresh air.

It was raining slightly but the wind was still warm, and I was informed for a third and last time that the weather was not particularly fine. The Nice Lady smelt of violets, a perfume that I seldom smell nowadays and that filled me with misplaced nostalgia. I love violets. I love them passionately, and I'm glad I'm never given them because they don't keep well in a vase. The scent prompted me to give a final wave to my departing visitor in her seat in the bus, and she waved back and smiled her unfathomable smile with her little lips and little eyes set in the long, narrow face.

Relieved but still baffled I made my way home, breathing in deep breaths of moist air. In the twilight the houses and gardens looked like ruins in a wilderness.

Our house – Hubert's house, I mean – looked foreign too. I felt as if I was on a visit there to my mother in law and could sense the cold streaming out towards me. That woman achieved everything she wanted in life, but me she was only able to banish for a couple of years, or one and a half to be precise. Hubert punished her cruelly for this, but I think unfairly, because although she may have been the instigator and he her unwitting instrument, it was still he who did the actual banishing. I have long since forgiven her, or better, have realised that there was nothing to forgive, seeing that she owed me nothing – neither friendship nor kindness. But Hubert cannot forgive her because he can't forgive himself. This is a misfortune for him, made no easier by the fact that it cannot be discussed.

I closed the gate behind me and walked up the path through the garden that is not my garden, to the house that is not my house. Only the loft is mine, and to be honest any other top-floor room would do just as well. It struck me what a strangely pleasant condition it is, to belong nowhere.

I cleared away the tea things and washed them up. From the sitting room I could still smell the scent of violets. The Nice Lady had come and gone, and it would be months before I saw her or thought of her again, but at any rate her visit had helped to pass the day. Now it was time I went up to the loft.

Once seated at my drawing table I wasted no thoughts on the nuthatch that had so unexpectedly turned into a lizard the day before, but started straight away on a buzzard. There was no question of a bird like that wearing a sociable air; I was simply anxious to prove to myself that I could still draw a bird. I thought back on my dream before it faded from my mind altogether, and it seemed to me that now I could actually feel what it was like to be a buzzard, wheeling around in circles high above the trees. I didn't want to force the creature into being something it wasn't, but I wanted to make it look at least as if it was happy in its solitude.

I drew for ten minutes and then I jumped up and started pacing to and fro. I couldn't see the buzzard at all, and this gave me such a shock that I fell into a deep depression. And I wasn't only depressed, I was completely shattered. Something terrible had happened to me: I couldn't see the buzzard and I couldn't see anything else either. I sank onto the sofa and cursed the person who had done this to me. Then I got up, went to the drawer, took out the envelope and began to read. There was nothing else he could do to harm me now.

February 17th

Now I know again what tears taste like. X cried. He looked like a dog that has been shot in the stomach. I know what that looks like too because once I saw one. I will never forget it. It was much worse than seeing X cry, because the dog had done nothing to deserve its suffering. Yesterday X broke our agreement. He leapt up from the table, came round to my side and started howling. I could see him howling but I couldn't move. He bent over me and his tears fell into my mouth. I wanted to comfort him but didn't know how. He wouldn't appreciate it anyway, he would take it as an offence. He dwells in a deep place where comfort cannot reach him. Sometimes I get the feeling that these words I cannot hear make their way to me through my skin, because lately I have been having bad dreams. I've never had dreams like that before, so cruel and violent. Hell is no fairy tale: X lives there and wants to drag me there with him. He doesn't want to be there alone. Last night I dreamt that he and I were shouting at one another through a wall of black glass, our faces pressed against it surface, our mouths wide open; then someone standing behind me laughed, and their laughter was so mocking that it woke me up. I'm not going near X any more: he has broken our pact, even though he didn't actually touch me. His tears have fallen on my lips. A fearful heat radiates from his body. I can't stand it any more, I am going to tell him our meetings are at an end.

March 1st

The thaw has set in. Water is running off the roof in rivulets. The cat has a huge belly that hangs from her backbone like a sack. It makes a sad sight, she's thinner than ever. The gamekeeper will drown the kittens, he always does. I know it's the wisest thing to do but all the same I don't like it. It looks as if he's fallen out with his lady friend recently: she's got green and brown marks all over her face. But she still stays around: like the dog, she's got nowhere else to go.

The stream is a mass of white froth; very soon the liverwort will start flowering again, the way it did last year. Except that it wasn't last year, it was last century. I am amazed I've kept so healthy: it's six months since I saw the sun; the valley is dripping damp; I eat little, sleep badly, and yet am in the best of health – not even a toothache. It's probably due to the fact that I'm always in the open air. It's not that I enjoy walking, it's just that I have to go somewhere or I get restless. The mountains encircle the house, dark and still like gaolers – they are bluish black today which means the wind is in the south. Sometimes they seem to me to be drawing closer together, closing me in a trap. One day they will crush me. And it's not only the mountains that give me this impression: I feel threats pressing in on me from all sides.

It's a long time since Hubert wrote. I imagine the apartment is already furnished and he is waiting for a miracle. It's up to me to work the miracle, I know, but I haven't a clue how to set about it. Maybe he's started to forget me – it's high time he did – but I suppose the presence of little Ferdinand keeps me alive in his memory.

Ferdinand is not mine any more, though: they have taken him away from me like the kittens from the cat. No, that's not true, *I* have taken him away from me; I have let him down and abandoned him. But why? It was obvious that a year and half's reflection would get me nowhere. There must be doctors who understand about these things, but the ones I saw knew nothing and were unable to help. Hubert has never had much faith in doctors, and now he has even less.

I still go and see X. He has made no further attempt to come near me and sits at the far end of the table, but his hands do terrible things: they no longer grasp at one another but crawl all over the place like two red crabs. It as if they are searching, blind and fumbling, for a victim that they cannot find.

March 4th

I've started doing crossword puzzles now. They work beautifully, I don't think about myself at all. It's so strange about words: the things we label have no idea that we have given them names in order to try to pin them down. It's like a butterfly collector with his specimens: 'you're a cabbage white and it's no use denying it because that's the way I classify you.' The little dead body makes no protest. Of course we don't really hold anything captive that way, we only imagine we do, in our megalomania. Which is why we are so afraid: who knows, one day the things we have named may lose their infinite patience and rise up against us in their true, horrendous forms. And these forms would indeed be horrendous because utterly alien to us. They could bury us under their mass, and we would forget their names and end up nameless ourselves. To be a human is a very chancy thing: perhaps without knowing it we're not really what people used to call 'humans' any more. Our courage is admirable, even though it may only consist in fear and stubbornness, but what purpose does it serve? I could solve twenty crossword puzzles a day if I felt like it, but the more I solved the less I would understand about the world.

The laurel is flowering. I don't pick any because I'm afraid the plant might cry out in pain and I wouldn't hear it. True, I don't remember ever hearing laurel cry out, but everything is possible, and every sound is possible to a person who cannot hear. Recently I've begun catching flies and silver fishes with a piece of paper and then flicking them out of the window, alive. My fingers refuse to squash them; no doubt they know the reason. To be squashed is so fearful and so final. I wonder everyone doesn't realise this. But then I too used to catch fish and wring chickens' necks: I made my hands kill because it was normal. Now I am no longer normal, but if I go back to being so, then perhaps my hands will be able to kill again. I wonder if want them too, though?

Yesterday I had a visitor – the first since I've been here. The pastor found his way here somehow. Presumably he'd have come sooner if he had seen me in church, but I never go to church. Even before, I only used to go when I was certain of being alone there; and I never prayed, I used to just sit in a pew and think of nothing. I like the atmosphere in churches, and the light coming through the stained glass windows.

I made some coffee for the pastor and we had a short conversation: that is, I talked and he wrote comforting sentences on my note pad. He found it difficult to put things about trials and hope and grace in writing, and I felt sorry for him. We were both a bit embarrassed. I didn't want to offend him because he is young and inexperienced and would take it hard. I doubt he will come back, however: even churchmen know when there is nothing they can do to help. He can't come just for the coffee either, because people would talk: a young pastor has to watch out for his reputation.

He looked so clean and zealous. I reckon he comes from another part of the country and is homesick. He complimented me on my drawings and I made him a present of a pair of finches. Before he left he cast a shy glance at my note pad, and I tore off the pages he had written and gave them back to him. He blushed, but took them, stuffed them in his pocket and left.

These pages I burned in the cellar like all the others. Then Hubert came home and I cooked supper. Hubert said he was glad the week was over. I would be glad myself were it not for the business of the buzzard. There can't be much more material left, surely. When the burner has consumed the last pages I can tell myself that it is all finished and done with. Maybe then I will be able to see things again and draw again. I certainly hope so because otherwise I hate to think what will become of me.

Later that evening we watched an old film, and fortunately I was able to doze through it. Then I went off to bed and Hubert stayed downstairs at his desk to read for an hour or so. I didn't hear him come upstairs, and I slept on until four, when the horrible drifting-in-the-darkness started again, but I'd rather not think about that.

Saturday

The moment I got up I could tell that the wind was still in the south. I felt very tired but at the same time wide awake. It was the feeling I used to get after a night of love with Hubert: dog tired but wide awake. That was such a long time ago, however, that I barely remember the nights; but the morning sensation is still clear in my mind, and the south wind has the same effect on me. It makes me work faster than usual – not gently and thoroughly the way the west wind does, not happily and busily the way the east wind does, not unwillingly, either, the way the north wind does when it makes my joints ache, but feverishly and fast. I tend to break glasses, and when I do I notice that my hands are slightly shaky.

Saturday morning is usually pretty hectic. We eat earlier than usual, and I have get the housework done first and do the shopping, waiting ages in each shop. People seem to stock up on Saturdays for the whole week. My appetite deserts me when I see what other housewives cram into their baskets: anyone would think they were preparing for a siege. It was ten o'clock when I got back to find the next envelope lying in the mailbox, bloated and yellow like a poisonous toad. Still wearing my coat I rushed up to the loft with it and hid it away. After which I sat in the kitchen for a full three minutes and shivered. When a plate I was holding fell from my hand I ascribed it to the effect of the south wind.

Hubert came back at midday; he made no comment on my veal cutlets which were tough and overcooked. I said nothing either because this was evidently one of those days when he was playing the part of the melancholy ascetic who cares nothing for food. As a matter of fact he never does comment on my veal

156

cutlets although they are usually delicious. I'm afraid this is a bad feminine trait – wanting to be praised for just doing your job as you should. Hubert works hard every day too and I never praise him for it. He probably wouldn't like it if I did, or would he? I'm not sure, but even if he did he wouldn't show it. His mother never praised him for anything, and this must have left its mark. I have done differently with Ferdinand and Ilse, and I hope they benefit from it.

Anyway, the veal cutlets were spoilt, and Hubert didn't notice, he was so deep in his role of ascetic, and I didn't care much either since I only cook for my family. If I lived alone I'd make do with a sandwich. The running of a middleclass household is all geared towards the comfort of men, and they work all their lives in order to be able to foot the bill. Admittedly there may be exceptions: some men may have wised up to the fact that you can live perfectly well without all that cooking and housekeeping, but Hubert is not one of them. His mother saw to that – his mother who never had to lift a finger and had a slave to do all the work.

I never speak of these things to Hubert, though: he might think I was shirking my duties. I never know how well he can take a joke. Sometimes we laugh together over the same things, and sometimes, when he feels his dignity is wounded, he doesn't laugh at all. And it's so difficult to know what constitutes a threat to a man's dignity. I have no dignity myself so mine is never wounded. Indeed I don't really know what dignity or honour are. There's not a trace of them in my make up – a fact I am careful to keep quiet about in order not to appear too weird. I'm always afraid of being judged weird: not on my own account but for Hubert's sake and Ferdiand's.

Once upon a time it was different. Hubert wasn't so keen on his dignity then, and we used to laugh a lot and invent games together – games he has now forgotten and that I myself can only vaguely recall. Can this be the same man who today sits for hours at his writing desk requiring not to be disturbed? If I could spy on those early days of ours through a keyhole they would no doubt seem very strange to me – so strange and remote that I would have to cry, and I can't remember how to.

I have changed too, but not that radically. When Ferdinand compliments me on my cooking, for instance, I could jump into the air for joy. Inside me there still lives a little girl who wants to warm her toes and dance around like all the other children. She is imprisoned there, though: the fate of all little girls who won't grow up. It's my own fault, really, if I can't resign myself to living in the present.

Roughly three times a year Ferdinand invites me out for a meal. This only happens when Hubert has a dinner engagement, but when it does the two of us eat and drink ourselves dizzy, while a malicious little imp inside me rejoices that all is being paid for by Madam Magistrate's money – she who begrudged me even a tiny slice of cake. We drink to the health of the older Ferdinand, and I hope for his sake that he too had occasions to celebrate, the way we are now doing. I think he must have done, because he was a wise man. Now he is merely a heap of ashes: he left instructions to be cremated, which I find a very neat solution for dealing with our remains. He would be happy if he could see his grandson who is so like him, and sit down with him and drink a glass of wine. He could still be alive today, but I don't think he would like it. Of course he wouldn't have had to lie in ward like Serafine, he'd have had a room to himself, but I doubt he'd have liked that either. His wife died in her own bed, in the arms of her old slave, and my parents and grandfather also died at home. A sister of my mother's came to take care of her – Marie, the one who went into the convent. Her name is now Sister Rosalie and I think it suits her. They must have chopped off that thick golden plait of hers; I bet my grandfather was livid. She was such a high-spirited girl and so pretty; I have never seen her since.

My mother looked beautiful and terrifying in her coffin. Terrifying because she had red patches on her cheeks as if she had been rouged, and green shadows round her eyes, which also looked painted on. I didn't recognize her as my mother. Someone had placed a white carnation in her folded hands. I felt sorry for the carnation because it had to be buried in the ground. I remember that well, and I remember also that my black dress was uncomfortable and scratchy. The nuns at school told me my mother was now in heaven with my father. I didn't believe them. I was fourteen, and at that age young people lose their faith. The truth was, my parents had never been present at all as far as I was concerned, so it didn't much bother me where they'd gone now.

The aunt wound up the household, and I went back to school, and the long summer holidays I spent as usual with my grandfather. It was a relief to me not to have to think about the cough-racked woman who had been my mother. Now I could begin to live and enjoy myself. My grandfather was always worried that I might have inherited the disease, and had me regularly examined, but I was healthy. My parents had hardly ever touched me: it was the best they could do for me and I find it generous on their part.

At home I had never been able to laugh because someone was always ill, but now at last I could: my grandfather taught me how. When his laughter stopped, so did mine. I learnt again with Hubert but not for long. The perfectly ordinary sound of a fire alarm going off at night was sufficient to turn me deaf. It might even have been the siren of a police car or an ambulance, I'm not sure. My father's night time coughing fits had never achieved this result and neither had the real sirens – the ones during the war. It was strange: the fire alarm or whatever it was went off, and I woke up in shock and I couldn't hear Hubert's voice any more. When it happened I wanted to die. My wanting to be alone and away from it all was a surrogate for death.

But then I arose from the dead again, and when you do that you belong nowhere any more. It is important to realise this and to understand it. At the time I didn't understand: I recovered my child – who was no longer mine – from Madam Magistrate's keeping, and took Hubert back from her as well, all the while wondering why these things didn't make me happy.

Because I wasn't happy; I felt guilty. But what are you to do when you aren't dead but only dead-apparent? The obvious answer is just to reoccupy the place you left vacant, but this doesn't really work either. In the new apartment I found a lipstick in the bathroom. We never mentioned this, Hubert and I. Who did it belong to? Who did I push aside, and who did he have to send away on my account? More guilt on his shoulders, placed there by me. A small guilt probably, but how can I judge? The fact remains that I drove someone else away. But things go as they will go and we must go on and live them out. Recriminations are of no avail to anyone, least of all to myself.

Today is the fourth Saturday in the month, and every fourth Saturday two old school friends of Hubert's come to play tarot with him. They used to be three, but the third died last year in an accident. So now they play three-sided tarot, which works almost as well. In actual fact they don't really play tarot at all, they play schools. In the past it used to make me a tiny bit jealous, but now I'm glad for Hubert's sake that he can still feel young and laugh. It's easy to tell they're school friends because they have nothing else in common. Had they just met up they wouldn't feel drawn to one another in the slightest. These two friends are called Malina and Gröschl and I still don't know their Christian names. Malina, an interior decorator by profession, is a tall, corpulent man; Gröschl, who is a teacher, is small and downtrodden and when he is talking to you, stares past you into a corner. I don't know whether this is due to shyness or whether he has some reason for avoiding my gaze. Malina is a ladies' man, and if ever we are left alone together he flirts. He can't help it, that is the way he is made. He has warm plump hands and the moist, conniving blue eyes of the born seducer.

I generally stay with them for about ten minutes only. They doff their official status together with their hats and coats and turn into a couple of adolescent boys: namely into the Malina and Gröschl who sat in the fifth row at school, close to Hubert and the other classmate who died. Their names switch suddenly to Maltzi and Groschi and they start calling Hubert Schnapsi, a name that can never have suited him. He likes them using this nickname, but not in my presence, so I leave the room as soon as I decently can. Not unwillingly either: I find it grotesque that there should be people who call Hubert Schnapsi.

There must be something amiss in the families of Malina and Gröschl because these meetings always take place in our house, never theirs. I leave some sandwiches out for them in the living room as a rule and disappear into the loft. It would sadden me should anything happen to either of them: two people can't play tarot.

After I'd washed up the lunch things I tried to convince Hubert to come out for a walk. He doesn't take enough exercise and this can't be good for him, so every weekend I chivvy him out into the fresh air. He resists as hard as he can, says he has work to do, or feels sleepy, or has a headache, but I am inflexible. Once he starts walking he is much faster than I am and I find it hard to keep up. Luckily, living as far out as we do, we can walk for a good ten minutes before meeting any traffic. If only Hubert wasn't so difficult to persuade: I am getting a bit sluggish myself nowadays and have to overcome my own reluctance as well as his. I some-times wonder if I do all this out of pure sense of duty, or whether a there isn't a bit of bossiness involved. If so, then bossiness is a positive trait.

So off we set, a middle aged married couple, hardly speaking to one another at all. This is not always the case. Sometimes Hubert chats to me about his practise, or asks me about my drawing, referring to it as my hobby. It can't interest him in the slightest, which is why I find his questions so touching. We hardly ever speak about the children. This sounds odd, but that's the way it is. The subject seems to unsettle Hubert: he's there for his children when they need him, but they very seldom do. Ilse comes to him when she needs help with her maths or more pocket money, and Ferdinand needs nothing. When he is at home with us, father and son talk about horse racing or cars or football. That is, Ferdinand does Hubert the favour of talking about these topics – all of them safe. They never touch on Hubert's work or Ferdinand's studies, about which they are truly informed. Of cars and horses and football they know next to nothing, and this guarantees a pleasant conversation.

Originally Ferdinand wanted to study archaeology. Hubert and I had nothing against the idea: Hubert, because he forced himself not to, and I, because I was so pleased that at last one of us was doing what they really wanted. But in the end Ferdinand himself decided against. 'You see, Mum,' he explained, 'with archaeology you can't make any money. You can only make a career of it if you have private means. And I know myself: I need money. Not because I want to keep it but because I want to spend it. I shall earn a lot of money, I know I shall, and then I shall live a really cushy life. Archaeology is a dream, and I must forget it. It's impossible to have a job I really like and that brings in big money as well, so I have opted for the money and the easy life. If I had to scrape by for years, the dream would die of its own accord. I'm not a hero or a fanatic; I like things that come easy. Surely you can understand that?'

What could I say? He knows what he has given up, and sometimes it torments him; but he will come to terms with this, the way the elder Ferdinand came to terms with his uncomfortable home life.

No, we never speak seriously about the children – they have slipped away from us and are ours no longer. Hubert has known this for a long time; I think he knows a lot more than I give him credit for. Today, though, we hardly spoke at all. The weather was fine again and the wind was letting up. The hills behind the city were blue and looked as if you could almost touch them, and the canals stank – a sure sign that the fine weather wouldn't last. Hubert always claims he doesn't feel the effects of the south wind but I don't believe him. It is the same with his dreams that he doesn't remember or care to remember. He tells himself: For-gotten dreams are not dreams at all, and weather isn't present if it has no effect on me. So we bickered a bit over this, both of us glad to have lighted at last on a nice neutral topic. I noticed how pleased Hubert was to be able to tease me a little, and I stuck to my guns so as to prolong his pleasure, and in the end the walk turned out a success. I pointed out to him ten dogs, two cats and a clump of early flowering coltsfoot growing on the edge of a sandpit. He was so amazed, it made me rather sad: what kind of a world does my husband live in, that things like dogs and cats and coltsfoot should amaze him?

At one point he took hold of my hand and we continued our walk like a pair of lovers – which I suppose we are really, in our strange way. Two minutes later, however, he evidently began to feel uncomfortable, as he freed his hand on the pretence of unbuttoning his coat. I think it goes against his dignity to walk hand in hand at his age. So then we proceeded side by side, more like good friends. Only friends know less about one another than we do, so for them it is easier still.

We were back home by three. I fixed us some coffee and Hubert made a beeline for his desk as if it was the only place in the world where he could find refuge. I brought him his coffee there, and then went into to the living room, determined to forget all about him for at least a couple of hours. Thinking about him all the time makes me exhausted. Hubert and Ferdinand and Ilse, and the living and the dead, and now, on top of them, this creature who has been persecuting me since Monday with thick yellow envelopes and about whom I know both too much and too little.

I sank onto the sofa, a thriller in my hand, and opened it at random somewhere in the middle. I read thrillers even though they don't interest me one bit. I never can remember whether I've read them or not, so in theory one thriller could last me a lifetime. I could achieve the same effect by drinking or taking pills, or by bidding some obliging person to come and hit me over the head every day with a hammer. This last would be the most efficient method, because pills and alcohol don't work quite so well as a remedy against my stupid habit of mulling things over, but thrillers are less harmful and don't leave hangovers. I like sleeping a lot, too, for the same reason. Sleep keeps me occupied because I dream. In my dreams everything is possible, and I like the feeling this gives me. I become quite a different person: I hang around strange dockland districts, perch in high treetops on some secret mission, waiting for exciting developments. Often I find myself scuttling through dusty attics, pursuers hot on my heels. Then at the last moment a partition comes down, hiding me from them and transporting me into a deep underground region where no one will ever find me, and I know I am safe. In my dreams I am very cunning, and avoid – easily, almost playfully – all the traps I am set.

Sometimes, though, but only very seldom, I have other kinds of dreams. Some of these I will never forget. Ten years ago, for example, I dreamed I was in a wide open landscape like a park in which big glass tanks were arranged, full of water. In them sat mermaids and mermen playing on harps and flutes. I couldn't hear through the glass what they were playing but I knew it was *the* true music, not destined for human ear. Their scaly tails shone like mother of pearl, and their long flowing hair floated on the surface of the water. They were beautiful. I stood and watched them in breathless rapture, but then suddenly I knew I wasn't meant to be there with these creatures. It grew dark and voice said: 'They have abandoned us; it is the end of the world.' I started to cry, and woke up to find Hubert shaking me by the shoulder. I had no idea where I was; everything around me was strange. The world had disappeared into the abyss. Hubert tried to comfort me, and I did my best to stop crying so as not to worry him, but the sense of an irreparable loss stayed with me for days afterwards.

If dreaming were a job I could have made a great career out of it. In fact all my gifts are pretty useless in this world where I am obliged to live. I have to adapt myself, and when adapting becomes too burdensome I read thrillers instead.

This time I didn't have to read long because no sooner had I started than the doorbell rang and in came the tarot players. Everything went off as usual. Gröschl stared past me at the umbrella stand; Malina lingered over his hand-kiss a moment too long, and everything about his body seemed to say: I like you and would willingly go to bed with you, but I can't because your husband is an old school pal. I gave him a friendly look, right into his moist blue eyes. I don't dislike him at all, he reminds me of a nice fat tomcat who has to purr now and again whether he wants to or not. Then I brought the sandwiches into the living room and left without a word. I could hear rough but cordial tones coming from three male throats. It is always like that – you would think it was an old boys' reunion and they hadn't met for years.

Now it was time for me to repair to the loft. I went up there, took the poisonous yellow toad out of the drawer and pored over it. (But that is a stupid comparison: toads are lovely friendly animals, and I will draw one soon to make amends.) I realized immediately that it was the last package, but even so my hands shook as I leafed through its pages. The south wind at work again, no doubt.

April 19th

Today I went to see X again. Something in him has changed, he seems to be elsewhere in his thoughts. We sat opposite one another as usual but this time he was silent. This has never happened before. He mumbled and moved his lips slightly from time to time, but seemed to be talking to himself. Every now and then he would raise his head and stare at me as if he was seeing me for the first time as I really am. It was not a comfortable feeling, to be seen by him in this way, but I waited patiently, going over in my mind how I was going to tell him that this was our last meeting: I had definitely decided to put an end to my visits.

Suddenly he stood up and went to make some coffee: he hasn't done that for quite a while. We drank the coffee and I was on the point of opening my mouth and telling him this would be the last time we drank coffee together, but then he started writing something on my note pad, so I waited to see what it was.

On the pad was written: 'I must leave here immediately. Come with me, I need you, you will never regret it.' The 'need' was underlined twice.

Now I could no longer say what I had been about to tell him. He looked like a starving dog begging for a bone. Sweat was pouring off his forehead and running down his face and neck but he didn't wipe it away.

I said, 'I have to think about it, give me time until tomorrow.'

He looked as if he could cry for joy. I felt sorry for him, very, but at the same time I loathed him more than ever before. In order not to have to see him any more I got up and left. He stood in the doorway and stared after me until I was out of sight.

When I reached home I buried myself in my chair and tried to reflect. I could no longer go back to Hubert: the miracle he expected from me had not happened. I could, of course, stay here for the rest of my life, sitting in my chair, meditating, illustrating books and walking the woods, but I have had enough of this. I can wait no longer for something – I know not what – to happen. Added to which, I can feel I am changing in some way I do not understand or like, and I don't want to have to be afraid of myself. X was quite sincere in his offer, of that I am sure. Perhaps I could get used to him, despite the fact that he looks like a homicidal maniac. Even homicidal maniacs need other people, especially someone into whose deaf ears they can scream every day. I am past thirty now, and I'm fed up with the gamekeeper and the valley and my gaolers, the mountains.

April 20th

I went for a walk in the woods and gave myself up entirely to my fruitless meditations. When I got back I still hadn't come to a decision, because all the time I had had before me the picture of X's hands, and it seemed to me impossible to have to see these hands for the rest of my life. But anything else I might do seemed equally

166

impossible. The best thing would be to sink into the earth and not exist anymore.

I climbed down the mountainside and took the little road that led to the house. The gamekeeper was standing outside, shooting bullets into a grey sack that lay near him on the ground. The sack was alive and moving in funny little jumps. I knew immediately what was inside it: the kittens' time was up. The gamekeeper took aim and the sack moved a short distance forwards; he aimed again, and yet again, and each time the grey thing crawled and shook. Not until the fourth shot did it stop moving. Then he turned and saw me, and with an uncomfortable kind of grin he picked the sack up and carried it round to the back of the house. The sack was red now and left a trail of drops on the ground.

I didn't go inside, instead I went straight back to X. My head was empty and I was freezing cold. I didn't care where X took me as long as it was away from here.

Now I have returned and am packing my case. But I am not going away with X anymore. Why I am writing this, I have no idea. Maybe it's because my grandfather used to say a job should always be finished off properly. If so, then that is what I am now doing.

When I got to X's I told him I would go with him, and he laughed. It was not a pretty sight. His hands were resting on the table, and the moment I saw them I knew I was mad and that I could never be in the same place as these hands. Then he suddenly stopped laughing and stared at me. I couldn't tell what was going through his mind because his eyes were completely black and covered with a silvery sheen, but he could see mine, and mine are easy to read.

I was so frightened I couldn't move. X looked down at his hands and laughed. Or perhaps it wasn't a laugh but only seemed like one. Then he watched them as, feeling their way blindly, they slowly crawled towards a glass of water that was lying nearby on the table, found it, and closed themselves around it tightly. The glass shattered and his hands started oozing blood. This reminded me of something and I began to scream. I was beside myself and didn't know what I was doing. X was still watching his hands, as if in amazement, but

167

then he stood up and started to come round the table towards me. His face was a deep red and his lips were moving fast; a rivulet of blood ran across the table.

It was then that the miracle happened – the miracle I had been supposed to work. I could hear. At first I didn't take in anything: all that was coming out of X's mouth were wild noises; but gradually, above the noises, I started to hear other sounds as well, and this at last gave me the strength to spring to my feet.

'There's someone coming!' I hissed at him. 'Keep away from me or I'll scream!'

The footsteps I had heard came nearer, and X stared at me in horror. I have never seen such terror in a human face.

At that point I rushed to the door and ran away without a backwards glance.

The gamekeeper was nowhere to be seen, so I hid in the wood behind the house until he came back. The air was full of noises, and I laughed and cried and bit my fingers. Now I will pack my things, and tomorrow morning I will leave on the first train. The gamekeeper will have to drive me to the station, though; I am not walking there alone along this solitary road.

So now for the sake of tidiness I have completed my task. Nobody can ever take little Ferdinand away from me again. It has all been a bad dream; I will forget it, as I will also forget what X told me before he realised I could hear again. Yes, I will definitely forget it.

Well, I was right about the last part: I truly do not remember a word. Certain things you have to forget if you are to go on living.

However there is still someone alive who remembers it and who cannot know that I have forgotten, indeed that I have never given a thought to the matter for years. He must have stolen my notes from my case that evening while I was arranging my departure with the gamekeeper. It would not have been difficult: he could have slipped into my room through the veranda under cover of darkness, five minutes would have been enough.

Where has he been all these years? And why has he never tried to contact me before? He has become a respectable citizen, no doubt, like so many others of his kind. And yet . . . does the sweat still drip off his forehead, I wonder, when he thinks of me?

I paced up and down the loft, considering all the possibilities. The least worrying is that the letters are intended simply as a threat or warning. This I may never discover, or may discover it later – years later or months later, or maybe in the next few days. But in any case it will be too late because he will never believe that I have forgotten everything. It's a new kind of cat-and-mouse game, evidently, but the mouse is not going to play. What difference does it make, another danger added to the rest? I could just as easily be run over by a car tomorrow, or be diagnosed as having a deadly disease. No, there is not the slightest cause for worry.

I went down into the cellar and something happened inside my head. I saw the figure of an old man who had finally decided to put an end to hatred and fear. He dried the last drops of sweat from his forehead and slipped a sheaf of papers into a yellow envelope. His lips moved, and I couldn't hear his words but I knew he was saying: 'Enough.' The image was hazy and disappeared straight away. It might have meant something or it might not.

I sat on the beer crate and thought about the buzzard and about the fact I could no longer draw birds. I shut my eyes and saw a shape forming in my mind but it was not that of a bird. I waited, and the creature grew clearer and began looking back at me out of golden-yellow eyes, and I realised to my astonishment that it was a dragon. I have always loved dragons, but since they are not real animals I have never ventured to draw one. Nor had one ever appeared to me before like this. A dragon is a creature that is quite all right on its own – solitude befits it. It's not born into the world like other animals, either, it is just suddenly there, fully grown, without knowing why. This you can tell from the permanently bewildered expression in its eyes.

I sat there in the cellar and went on thinking of nothing but the dragon. I tried to hold fast to its image, as it had first appeared to me. It seemed the right thing to do and I found it very enjoyable. These are the only things I really understand about. The world is a labyrinth where I shall never find my way around, not with this head of mine that is made for conjuring up images, and not for thinking rational thoughts. I suddenly felt very tired, but not at all frightened. I could see the dragon very clearly now: it had wonderful yellow eyes that looked at me with total innocence and candour. What am I? They seemed to say. What am I?

'You are a dragon,' I told it, 'and that is an unusual thing to be because dragons are not supposed to exist. But you don't know that, and you exist all right because I can see you.'

I made my way up to the loft again – slowly because I was feeling exhausted. I flung the window open and the south wind blew in and cleared the room of everything that had no right to be there. I sat down and started drawing my dragon. It took shape effortlessly. When I had sketched the outline it looked absolutely right, and I felt happier than I had been for ages. I lay down on the battered old sofa and closed my eyes. I could hear no noises coming from downstairs. I thought of nothing – neither of the tarot players, nor of Ilse nor Ferdinand, nor the living nor the dead, not even of the unfortunate man who might be planning evil against me. At long last I thought of nothing: my head was beautifully empty and silent. That is how I imagine heaven. I closed my eyes and no pictures appeared, no images, just a blank. I was a hollow shell, enclosing nothing. I didn't fall asleep, I merely lay there in the silent void, totally at peace.

Later that evening, when I went to bed, I went to sleep immediately. I didn't dream, not that I remember.

Sunday

When I woke up it was Sunday again. Hubert was rustling the pages of his book –the history of the battle of Ebelsberg. He had already opened the curtains and the room was bright – as bright as you could expect on a February morning. The tree – the acacia, elm, or aspen or whatever it is – stood there in the damp air like a drawing in black pencil.

Hubert laid aside his book and said, 'Good morning', and kissed me on the cheek. He saw where I was looking and added, 'Today one can see very clearly that it's an agacia.'

I couldn't myself. To me it could just as easily be an aspen or an elm. It must have rained during the night because the tree was so dark and wet. A bird came and settled in it, then another, then a third: blackbirds, greenfinches, whatever, I can't tell without my glasses. It was a Sunday like every other.

Hubert said: 'Every time one bird alights another flies off, now isn't that strange.'

I made no reply and he went back to his book. I was pleased to see the tree standing in its usual place. Soon the cloud business would start up again, and it would lull me back to sleep.

Hubert said: 'The weather must have changed, my corn is hurting again.'

'Poor you,' I said. 'Shall I bring you breakfast in bed for a change?'

He pulled himself bolt upright, and I noticed his eyelids were a shade red around the rims: that came from smoking too much at the card table. 'Whatever for?' He answered, slightly indignant. 'You know I never eat breakfast in bed.'

'Well, you could,' I said, 'just this once'.

'I could but I won't,' he said. 'All my life I have had breakfast at the table.'

171

'Exactly,' I said. And then: 'It was just an idea.'

Pacified, he sank back and went on with his reading, and I lay there and watched the tree transform itself once more into a two dimensional object. We shall never know whether it is an elm or an aspen or an acacia, or what it is. Today, however, I didn't feel in need of its magic, so instead of going back to sleep I got up and began my day. My only concern was to get through it as fittingly as possible and then, when evening came, to go back to my dragon. For a moment I was afraid it might have changed over-night, but the fear soon passed.

'So?' Hubert asked. 'What are we going to do today?'

'Ferdinand is coming to lunch,' I said firmly, 'and afterwards we're going for a walk, and then to the War Museum.'

This shortened version of our game didn't seem to satisfy him; he shook his head worriedly and resumed his reading. I couldn't follow the rules today, though, I was far too excited.

The day passed as planned. Ferdinand arrived round about eleven and chatted to his father about winter sports and cars and football. Over lunch he praised my apple fritters, and I was pleased about this but in a detached kind of way. Afterwards we had coffee, and Ferdinand went on chatting to us for a while about nothing in particular, then said goodbye and kissed me on the cheek. He smelt young and delicious, and it occurred to me how strange it is that he has grown into a man and is no longer the little child whose heart I once wanted to re-conquer.

Today I marched Hubert round the block three times, because the weather was really not nice enough for a proper walk, and then we drove to the War Museum. Hubert made straight for the photograph section in search of his presumed father, and I just wandered aimlessly around. I admired some models of old ships, in particular the steam frigate 'Novara', and then spent a long time in front of the uniformed dummies – Croats, and halberdiers, and the soldiers of Prince Eugene. Since there was no one else around, I spoke to them. They couldn't hear me, and this reminded me of something I had meant to forget. So I left them there in their glass cases and made my way to the big Turkish tent.

The same as always, but I wasn't bored: I am never bored by the War Museum. And if there is something not quite normal in that, who cares?

Later on I met up with Hubert in the foyer. He had already bought himself a booklet on the battle of Dürstein-Loiben, 1805, and looked very relaxed and happy.

'You're sure now, then, that it's your father?' I asked him.

'Pretty sure,' he replied. 'Of course, I might have to take another look: these photographs need examining several times over.'

'Yes,' I said. 'I agree, they need examining several times over.'

Then we drove home. Hubert sat down at his desk and buried himself in the battle of Dürstein-Loiben; I could tell he had forgotten all about me. I felt very fond of him at that moment, but this he will never know. Truly, I felt very fond of him. I was moved by the sight of his back and the nape of his neck: they reminded me of the Little Tin Soldier.

There was no time, however, for further admiration: I had to go and attend to my dragon.

'See you later, Hubert,' I said. Quite unnecessary, but he murmured a polite reply without turning round. If one day I am not here anymore, I know he will miss me badly, even though he has no time for me at present.

I went upstairs to the loft, tripping over the last step which is a bit worn. I was walking with my eyes shut, in order to see more clearly the innocent, yellow eyes of the dragon.